Spirit
RIDING FREE

Lucky and the Mustangs of Miradero

SUZANNE SELFORS

Little, Brown and Company
New York Boston

Little, Brown and Company
Hachette Book Group
1290 Avenue of the Americas, New York, NY 10104
Visit us at lb-kids.com

First Edition: October 2017

Little, Brown and Company is a division of Hachette Book Group, Inc. The Little, Brown name and logo are trademarks of Hachette Book Group, Inc.

The publisher is not responsible for websites (or their content) that are not owned by the publisher.

Library of Congress Control Number: 2017953614

ISBNs: 978-0-316-50623-6 (paper over board), 978-0-316-55790-0 (ebook)

Printed in the United States of America

LSC-C

10 9 8 7 6 5 4 3 2 1

OFFICIAL
MARK OF
SPIRIT

For my mother, Marilyn,
and my sister, Laurie,
who have always lived their lives
as free spirits.

Introduction

The wild stallion stood at the edge of the canyon, ears alert, face pressed into the breeze. Above, the autumn sky glowed, a sheet of perfect blue, broken only by the swooping arc of a kestrel. Below, the river flowed, twisting and churning, making music as water met rock. The day was perfect for grazing. The stallion shook a fly off his nose, then dipped his head and tugged at a clump of grass.

His mustang herd grazed alongside. A few of the older, more experienced horses nibbled barrel cactus fruit, careful to avoid the barbs. A mare continued to graze, while patiently nursing her foal. This was how the herd spent its days, constantly feeding in order to build up fat storage for winter. Once the weather turned cold and the grasses died back, the members of the herd would be forced to walk farther and farther each day to find enough food to fill their bellies. But for now, all was well.

The foal stopped nursing, distracted by a butterfly. He was joined by another, a filly, who seemed equally fascinated by the winged creature. Butterflies were in abundance this time of year, thanks to flowering desert broom. Wide-eyed and mesmerized, the pair traipsed after the butterfly. At their age, each day brought something new to see, to smell, and to taste. Everything was an adventure. *And* a distraction.

The stallion snorted at the youngsters. Too much time playing and not enough time eating would not bode well. But he understood. He wanted to gallop through the canyon, kicking up clouds of red dirt in his wake. But he remembered last winter, when the grasses had all died. He remembered the emptiness in his stomach. He fought the urge to gallop and continued grazing.

For something felt different on this day. A cool, crisp note hung in the air. It was a note that all animals recognized.

Winter would come early.

Part One

1

Most of the time, days are ordinary, filled with familiar sights, sounds, and practiced routines. But for Lucky Esperanza Navarro Prescott, a twelve-year-old girl who'd recently moved from the cobbled streets and architectural wonders of the city to the wide open range of the West, most days were of the *extra*ordinary variety.

And such was this day. She had absolutely no idea what to expect. Which made her bouncy with anticipation. "Are you ready? Come on, let's go," she urged as she stood in the open doorway—a threshold between home and adventure.

"I've never been to a harvest festival," said Lucky's father, Jim Prescott, as he set a leather hat on his head. Like his daughter, his voice brimmed with excited curiosity.

"Neither have I," said Cora Prescott, Lucky's aunt. She also set a hat on her head, only this one was adorned with a papier-mâché apple and a cluster of papier-mâché cherries, all painted bright red. She'd special-ordered the bonnet from a renowned haberdashery in New York City. It had arrived at the train station in a box marked SPECIAL DELIVERY. "What do you think?" Cora asked, pushing back her blond hair and striking a serious pose.

"You look very pretty," Jim told her.

"You sure do," Lucky said.

Cora smiled as she tied the ribbon beneath her chin. "Thank you." Appearances were important to Cora, for she believed that proper grooming was a sign of taking pride in oneself. Cora had been raised among debutantes and socialites who cared about etiquette and manners. But since moving out West, Cora had changed. No longer were her days spent in Parisian-inspired cafés nibbling crustless sandwiches, or in ornate art museums discussing the latest trends in landscape painting. These days she cut wood, pumped water, and fed chickens—which explained the color in her cheeks and the flecks of dirt beneath her fingernails.

"I just hope a flock of crows doesn't attack your head," Lucky said, pointing to the cherries.

Cora's hand flew to the top of her hat. "Oh dear. Do you think?"

Lucky immediately regretted her comment. If Cora

went upstairs to choose a totally different, fruit-free bonnet, the whole morning could be stalled. They'd *never* get to the harvest festival. "I'm just kidding," Lucky said with a wave. "Crows know the difference between real cherries and fake cherries. Can we go now?"

"Would you like me to carry those?" Jim asked, pointing to a basket that sat on the table. The basket contained three jars of Cora's homemade raspberry jam.

"Oh yes, thank you. I'm going to enter them in the canning contest at the festival. Next year I might try pickles."

"Who would have thought?" Jim teased as he grabbed the basket. "This time last year you were fund raising for the new wing at the art museum, and here you are, mashing berries and putting them into jars."

"It's a lot more complicated than just *mashing berries*," Cora corrected with pursed lips. She ran her fingers over her ever-present strand of pearls. "You have to consider the particular qualities of the fruit. And you don't just put them into jars, Jim. You have to abide by the strict rules of preservation. It's always good to learn new skills. If there's one thing I am, it's *adaptable*." This was a true statement. Ever so slowly, the layers of city expectations were peeling off Cora, revealing something more colorful beneath. She was definitely a work in progress.

But a few of Cora's tendencies were taking longer to change. She put her hands on her hips and gave Lucky a look of disbelief. "Is *that* what you're wearing to the harvest festival?"

Lucky frowned. "Yes."

While her aunt wore a crisply ironed skirt, high-collared blouse, and heeled boots, Lucky wore her most comfortable pants and a flannel shirt. And she rarely went anywhere without her signature boots: brown leather with embossed red flames and shooting stars. The boots had belonged to her departed mother. They were one of Lucky's most beloved possessions, and they'd conformed to her feet as naturally as a cocoon wraps around its occupant.

"Well, I know better than to try to change your mind, but at least let me tie back your hair," Cora insisted. Lucky agreed, mostly to avoid a nose-to-nose argument with her equally stubborn aunt. She turned around and bowed her head. Cora gathered Lucky's long brown hair and tied it with a ribbon. "That's better."

"Can we go *now*?"

"We could," Jim said. "Unless you think I also need a ribbon in my hair?"

"Dad!"

Jim chuckled. "Yes, by all means, let's go."

"Finally!" Lucky flew onto the front porch and scrambled down the steps, stomping so loudly she startled a chipmunk up a tree.

It was a short walk to town. The Prescott house had been built on a hill, which provided a sweeping view of the landscape. Autumn was a colorful time of year in Miradero. The trees were turning, with leaves of yellow, orange, and red. Desert broom seemed to be everywhere. According to Doc Wilkins, desert broom was a nuisance for many of the town's residents, causing sneezing and itchy, watery eyes. But the seeds certainly looked pretty as they floated through the air in billowy tufts, like clouds. Patches of soapberry and hackberry trees added splashes of color against the background of flat-topped red mountains. While the view from their home back in the city had been rows of buildings, here the sky went on forever.

"This is the biggest festival in Miradero," Jim told

them. "Everyone has taken the day off from work. Even JP & Sons is closed." *JP* stood for James Prescott Sr., Lucky's grandfather. He was the owner of the railroad and, thus, well known throughout the region. Jim was the "sons" part of the equation, and he'd been sent to Miradero to oversee the railroad's expansion.

Because the festival was such a popular event, Lucky's teacher had even assigned her students homework. "Miss Flores is making us write a report about what we do today," Lucky said as she walked between her father and aunt. Miss Flores was Lucky's teacher, and she was quite fond of assigning reports. But in this instance, Lucky didn't mind. Not really. Something exciting was bound to happen at the festival, for there was never a dull moment in these parts. And then she'd have the perfect story for her essay.

They walked toward Main Street. If people's personalities could be revealed by the way they walked, it was certainly true of this trio. Lucky's steps were lively and quick, her arms swaying, her head turning left and right, for she was curious about everything. Cora's steps were determined and evenly paced, her hands clutching a small purse, her chin held high. Jim, with his long legs, strode in an easygoing manner, the basket tucked under his arm. No longer buttoned up in wool suits and vests, Jim had adopted the more casual style of the West. And while he used to smell like an office—a combination of coffee and dust, ink and paper—Lucky noticed new scents clinging to him: fresh air and dirt, from all the time he now spent outdoors.

Lucky adored her father, and likewise, he adored her. When he broke the news that he was moving to Miradero to oversee the work of JP & Sons, there'd been immense pressure from Lucky's grandfather and from Aunt Cora to keep Lucky in the city, where she could continue her private education at one of the nation's top schools for young ladies. But Lucky and Jim refused to be separated, and eventually, love won. Even Cora agreed to join them, which had surprised everyone!

"Lucky, look!" Jim pointed at a nearby hill.

Lucky's gaze traveled across the road, past an old barn, past a cluster of soapberry trees, until it rested on a pair of warm brown eyes.

2

"Spirit!" Lucky called.

Neither Jim nor Cora tried to stop Lucky as she scampered away. Back in the city, she was never allowed to set out by herself. But here in Miradero, she'd been set free! Free from the confines of her starched school uniform. Free from the rules of her uppity finishing school. In Miradero, Lucky ran. She explored. And most especially—she rode!

Upon reaching the top of the hill, she threw her arms around the stallion's neck. He was a buckskin mustang, with a black mane and black tail. His lower legs were also black.

"Hello," she said. He dipped his head forward, then down, exhaling a deep, fluttering breath through his nostrils. The warm air tickled her face and neck. She brushed his forelock from his eyes. Never would she forget the first time she saw him. She was on the train when he'd raced by, trying to outrun a pair of *mesteñeros* and their ropes. But they'd caught him and brought him to a ramada owned by a man named Al Granger. Mr. Granger and his men had tried to break Spirit, but they'd failed. When Mr. Granger's daughter, Pru, and her best friend, Abigail, rode into a dangerous canyon, Spirit and Lucky had saved their lives. In gratitude, Mr. Granger gave Spirit to Lucky. But Lucky knew she could never "keep" such a magnificent creature. So she gave him his freedom.

Which he'd reclaimed, but not entirely.

For Spirit was now a common sight in town, returning often to see Lucky and to ride with her. Spirit held a special status with the townsfolk, like a houseguest who comes and goes. No one in Miradero would try to capture or break him ever again.

"I bet you want to go for a ride," Lucky said as she ran her hand down his muzzle. He raised his head, his ears pricked in her direction. Ride? Of course he wanted to ride. Riding was their favorite thing to do. But the timing was bad. She looked over her shoulder. Her father and aunt were waiting.

"Lucky!" Jim called.

"I'm sorry, Spirit, I can't ride this morning," Lucky told him. It nearly broke her heart to say those words. "I'm going to the harvest festival." She pointed down Main Street, which was lined with tents and tables. The faint sound of a fiddle drifted in the breeze. "You want to come with me?" She tugged on his mane. His legs stiffened. Though he'd become used to Lucky's family and friends, he was still wild at heart and didn't like mingling with crowds of people. "I understand," Lucky said. "Let's ride later?"

He snorted at her, which she knew meant *okay*. She kissed his cheek. "I love you so much," she whispered. He pushed her playfully with his head, then turned and galloped away.

"You and that horse," Cora said as Lucky returned. "Why can't you ride one of those miniature ponies that Pastor Perkins keeps? If you fall off one of those, you might bruise your tailbone. But if you fall off Spirit, well…" She frowned. "Why did you have to choose a *wild horse*?"

"He chose me," Lucky said. Then she hugged her aunt. "You worry too much."

"Of course I do. My most important job is to look after you." Cora proudly adjusted her hat. She took *all* her jobs very seriously.

"Hey, I thought looking after Lucky was *my* job," Jim said with a chuckle.

"I don't need looking after," Lucky insisted.

A crowd had gathered at the end of Main Street. A

bright-yellow ribbon hung across the street, tied to posts on either side. Mayor Gutierrez, being short in stature, had climbed onto a stool so everyone could see him. He wore a gray waistcoat and a black bowler hat. "Welcome, welcome!" he called, his arms waving. "Gather 'round, gather 'round. It's time to open the festival!" Applause and cheers filled the air. Jim squeezed Lucky's arm. They shared a smile. A shiver of anticipation darted up Lucky's back. What was going to happen next?

The mayor scratched his enormous mustache, waiting for the cheering to subside. Then he puffed out his chest and continued. "We've gathered on this day to celebrate the autumn abundance of Miradero, which is growing every year, thanks to all the efforts I have made on your behalf." He paused, a huge smile plastered on his face. "Efforts I have made as your mayor." He paused again. Did he want applause? Lucky shuffled in place. A frog croaked.

"We should thank the railroad!" someone hollered.

The mayor cleared his throat. "Yes, yes, of course. JP & Sons Railroad has been a huge benefit to our little town." People turned and looked at Jim. A round of applause arose. Jim's cheeks turned red. Not one for attention, he waved his hands, trying to silence the applause. Mayor Gutierrez's smile faded slightly. He adjusted his fancy waistcoat, then coughed loudly for attention. "As your mayor, I will continue to work with the railroad to make sure that Miradero grows and prospers. For your success is my success." He beamed another smile, then pulled a piece of paper from his vest pocket. "There is certainly a lot to do today. Don't miss the zucchini races, which will be held at two o'clock in front of Winthrop's General Store. Be sure to check out Alice Crumb's giant pumpkin, which is on exhibit next to Town Hall. It's the largest pumpkin ever grown in Miradero, isn't that right, Alice?"

"Biggest one yet!" Alice Crumb hollered from the center of the crowd. "I fertilized it with rabbit droppin's. That's the best stuff for growing gourds and such. If you don't got rabbit droppin's, then you can use goat droppin's, but they don't work so good."

The mayor, who was not a farmer nor inclined to outdoor labor of any sort, smiled politely. "That's very interesting. As you know, the mayor's office fully supports the farmers of Miradero." He continued reading from his notes. "Speaking of goats, there are three new babies in the petting area. Be sure to stop by Mary Pat and Bianca's apple cider stand. The Miradero Ladies'

Aid Society is selling buttered corn on the cob. And this year, the cakewalk tickets are twenty-five cents and will raise money for the Miradero church, which is badly in need of some repair work due to *an unfortunate incident*." He paused and looked directly at a little redheaded boy named Snips Stone. Lucky hadn't witnessed the *unfortunate incident* but had heard all about it. Snips's donkey, Señor Carrots, had a reputation for breaking out of his yard and getting into trouble. On this particular occasion, he'd wandered into the church, got stuck, then kicked his way free, damaging one of the pews.

"Señor Carrots is very, very sorry," Snips called from the front of the crowd. "But there's no sign on the door that says 'No Donkeys Allowed'."

"There is now!" someone hollered. A few people laughed.

The mayor shot Snips another long look. Then he raised his hands again and his big politician's smile returned. "Without further ado, my lovely daughter, Maricela, our harvest princess, will now cut the ceremonial ribbon."

Maricela.

Lucky narrowed her eyes. Maricela Gutierrez had been the first girl to greet Lucky when she'd arrived in Miradero last spring. Like Aunt Cora, Maricela's mother had been raised in the city and attempted to maintain decorum in dress and manners. Lucky had been happy to meet a girl her own age, and she'd been willing to be friends. But Maricela had proved, time and time again, to be an unpleasant snob, holding herself above everyone else.

Today she wore her favorite yellow dress and a sash that read HARVEST PRINCESS. She also wore a crown of woven flowers. "Thank you, thank you," she said, curtsying and waving to the crowd. People politely applauded. She continued to curtsy even after the applause stopped. Lucky rolled her eyes. Maricela really loved being the center of attention.

Mayor Gutierrez handed her a pair of scissors. With a dramatic flourish, she swept the scissors through the air, then cut the ribbon. But nothing happened. "They're not working," she grumbled as she tried to cut the ribbon again and again. "They're too dull!" Both she and her father turned their backs to the crowd and a whispered argument commenced. Everyone leaned forward to listen.

"Why didn't you get a better pair of scissors?"

"Those are the best scissors I could find. Let me do it."

"No. *I'm* the harvest princess. This is *my* moment."
Their voices grew louder.

"Give me those scissors!"

"Stop it! Let go!"

"Be careful! Scissors are dangerous!"

"Dad! You're ruining everything!"

After a brief wrestling match, the ribbon was finally cut. Both the mayor and his daughter turned back toward the crowd and smiled just in time to have their photo taken. Maricela curtsied again. Mayor Gutierrez climbed back onto the stool, stuck a finger in the air, and decreed, "The festival has begun!"

Lucky nearly jumped out of her boots. Finally!

3

"*Lucky!*"

"Hey, Lucky!"

Lucky didn't need to spin around to see who was calling her name. She knew those voices by heart. They belonged to her new best friends, Pru Granger and Abigail Stone. In fact, the girls had started calling themselves the PALs, which stood for their names: Pru, Abigail, and Lucky. She looked beseechingly at her father. "Can I go join them?" she asked. Jim nodded and handed her a one-dollar coin. "Thanks!"

"Don't eat too many sweets," Cora said. "And don't…"

Lucky cringed. Certainly there'd be a long list of things. *Don't* run too fast. *Don't* get lost. *Don't* fall in a hole. But Cora didn't finish her sentence. She took a long breath, then said, "Have fun." Lucky knew it took a lot of self-control for Cora to hold back, so she gave her a big hug.

"See you later," Lucky said, then hurried away to join her friends.

And there it was, her newfound freedom. Back in Philadelphia, Lucky had been chaperoned everywhere she went. Her housekeeper, Mrs. MacFinn, walked her to school. During inclement weather, the family butler, Mr. MacFinn, drove her in the carriage. Lucky never walked the city streets alone. But everything was different in Miradero. Lucky had tasted freedom and she was hooked!

Pru and Abigail smiled as Lucky ran up to them. Though they shared a keen love for horses and all things horse related, the two girls were quite opposite in other ways. Pru, with her long black hair, lanky physique, and outgoing temperament. Abigail, with her cropped blond hair, apple cheeks, and sweet disposition. Pru peered over Lucky's shoulder and said, "Why is she still waving?" referring to Maricela, who was now standing on the stool. "Does she think she's an actual princess?"

"She does look very pretty in that sash and crown," Abigail said.

Pru folded her arms tightly. "Maricela's been harvest princess three years in a row. Her mom made that sash."

Lucky wondered about the sour expression on Pru's face. "Do *you* want to be harvest princess?"

"No way," Pru said, sticking out her tongue as if that idea tasted bad. "I'm just saying, Maricela's acting so hoity-toity. Nobody got to vote. Her parents made up the whole harvest princess thing."

As far as Lucky knew, Pru and Maricela had never gotten along. And when Pru got into a bad mood, it was difficult to get her out. So Lucky tried to change the subject. "This is my first harvest festival. What should we do first?"

Abigail's blue eyes lit up. "Let's go see the baby goats!"

Pru's demeanor instantly changed. "I love baby goats!"

And so they set out to see every inch of the festival, for there was nothing better than a day spent exploring with good friends. Abigail—sweet, friendly, and always looking at the good side of things. Pru—fierce, brave, and competitive to her core. And Lucky—curious, eager, and happy to be on her own.

The morning activities proceeded at a brisk trot. The goats were adorable, especially the smallest one, which stood on its hind legs and nibbled on Lucky's ribbon. At the apple-bobbing tent, the girls laughed when their faces and hair got wet. They played ringtoss and helped some of the younger kids on the pony rides. Abigail bought a bag of caramel corn to share and Pru got some candy apples. While they nibbled corn on the cob, they strolled between the craft booths.

"Why, hello there, young miss. I remember you." A small, thin man stood beneath a sign that read DR. MERRIWEATHER'S MEDICINAL TONICS. Lucky had met him during her train ride. "My, my, don't you look different these days? Looks like the West suits you."

"It does," Lucky told him proudly.

"And what about that lovely aunt of yours?" His already-round eyes got even rounder. "Does the West suit her, too?"

Lucky glanced up and down the street and spotted Cora chatting with a few women from the Miradero Ladies' Aid Society. They were deep in conversation. "Yes, I think it does."

"I'd certainly like to show her my new batch of stomach tonic." He held up a small brown bottle. "This special tonic, to which I hold the exclusive patent, helps the most delicate of stomachs to digest the gassiest of foods. It also takes the itch out of flea bites and removes rust from frying pans. Would you like to give it a try?" He opened the bottle and held it out. It stunk like boiled cabbage.

"No, thank you," Lucky told him, resisting the urge to plug her nose. "My stomach is just fine."

"Abigail, it's time for the races!" Abigail's little brother, Snips, tugged on his sister's sleeve.

"Wow, is it two o'clock already?" Lucky asked with surprise. She guessed the adage that "time flies when you're having fun" was true.

"You promised to watch Señor Carrots while I race," Snips reminded his sister.

"But he always bites me," Abigail said. "Why can't you leave him at home?"

"I can't leave him. He gets lonely."

Señor Carrots, who'd bitten half the town population and who seemed intent on biting the other half, pushed against Snips. He was trying to reach an object that Snips held in his hands. "He wants to eat it," Snips complained. "Bad Señor Carrots!"

Lucky took a closer look at the object. It was a green zucchini, but four wooden wheels had been inserted into it and the center had been hollowed. "What is that?" she asked.

"It's a zucchini wagon," Abigail explained. "For the zucchini race."

"I even got a driver." Snips pointed to a dead beetle he'd stuck inside.

Lucky laughed. "Never seen *that* before."

"Señor Carrots likes you," Snips told Lucky. "Will you please hold him while I race?"

Most people would not get near the notorious donkey, but he'd always been fond of Lucky.

"Please," Snips begged, turning his pudgy little face up at Lucky and sticking out his lower lip.

"Sure." She grabbed the donkey's rope. "Don't give me any trouble," she told him, shaking a finger. He brayed, displaying his large teeth. Then he head-butted her, but not so hard that she lost her balance. She head-butted him back.

The temporary racetrack consisted of an inclined wooden ramp. At the top was a starting line, at the bottom, a finish line. The youngest members of Miradero climbed onto a bench and lined up their zucchinis. "They're supposed to make the wagons themselves, but you can tell which ones the parents made," Pru whispered to Lucky. Lucky snickered, for it was obviously true. And not everyone had followed the zucchini rule. One kid had used a small pumpkin.

Another had used a potato. No one seemed to care that the rules had been stretched, which was one of the things Lucky loved about Miradero.

Jim had been chosen to judge the competition. He raised a flag, then hollered, "Ready. Set. *Go!*" Jim waved the flag and the kids gave their zucchinis a push. Some of the vegetable wagons rolled down the ramp; others wobbled. A few soared out of their lanes, crashing to the ground in a splatter of pulp and seeds. There were tears. There was disappointment. And there was glory. "The winner is"—Jim made a drumroll sound—"Snips Stone!"

Lucky started clapping, and just as she released her grip on Señor Carrots's rope, the donkey bolted forward and ate the pumpkin wagon before she could stop him. "Señor Carrots!" she hollered.

"Señor Carrots is very, very sorry," Snips said. But the donkey didn't look sorry. He licked his lips, then eyed a yellow zucchini. The pumpkin's owner was happy with her second-place ribbon, so there were no more tears.

Next came the flour-sack race. While Pru raced ahead of everyone, easily taking the lead, Lucky and Abigail bumped into each other, ending up in a big heap of laughter. As Lucky climbed out of her sack, she found her aunt standing over them. Lucky expected a lecture about dirt, but instead, Cora smiled. "I won third place for my jam." She held up a white ribbon.

"Congratulations, Miss Prescott," Abigail said.

"Yeah, that's really great, Aunt Cora." Lucky hadn't seen her aunt looking this proud since she'd taught herself how to make a chocolate soufflé in a wood-burning oven.

"Hey, let's go do the cakewalk," Pru said as she joined them. They headed to the churchyard, where an array of cakes sat on a table. The girls each bought a ticket from Mrs. Perkins, the pastor's wife.

"Abigail's gonna win," Pru said.

"How do you know?" Lucky asked.

"Because she wins a cake every year."

Abigail shrugged. "It's true. Last year I won a strawberry cake with whipped cream filling."

"Abigail has the best luck of anyone I've ever met," Pru said.

Lucky smiled wickedly. "Don't be so sure. Remember, my name *is* luck."

Mrs. Perkins played the fiddle. As music filled the air, the ticket holders marched in a circle. When the music stopped, they each turned over the rock closest to them. "I won!" Abigail shouted, holding up her rock, which had been painted with the word *Cake*. Lucky and Pru clapped. Abigail chose a chocolate cake with chocolate icing and raspberry filling. She carried her prize to a patch of grass beneath an old walnut tree. "How are we going to eat this?" she asked as the PALs sat in the grass.

Pru shrugged. "With our hands?"

"Aunt Cora would die if she caught me eating cake with my hands," Lucky told them.

Five minutes later, with chocolate on their faces and fingers, the PALs moaned.

"Maybe we shouldn't have eaten caramel corn, candy apples, *and* cake," Lucky said. Cora's voice chirped in her ears. *Don't eat too many sweets!*

"Yeah, I don't feel so good," Pru complained.

"I feel sick," Abigail moaned.

They lay down, side by side, and stared at the sky that shimmered between the walnut tree's leaves, which were turning yellow. Lucky closed her eyes, hoping the cramp in her stomach would go away. She wondered what Spirit was doing. Was he racing across the prairie with his herd? Was he napping in a pool of autumn sunshine? Oh, why had she eaten so much cake?

"Hello, Lucky. Hello, Abigail."

Lucky's eyes flew open. Maricela stood over her. Lucky sat up. "Did you see me cut the ribbon?" Maricela asked. She adjusted her crown. The flowers were starting to droop.

"Yeah, I did," Lucky said.

Abigail also sat up. "I like your sash," she said sweetly.

"Oh thanks. Well, guess what?" Maricela's yellow dress billowed as she did a twirl. "I'm going to be in the newspaper. That's right. On account of the fact that I'm the harvest princess. There's going to be an entire article about *moi*." She glanced at Pru. "*Moi* is French. It means 'me.'" Pru groaned and rolled onto her side, facing away from Maricela.

Lucky wondered why Maricela was making such a big deal. The *Miradero Gazette* was a tiny paper, about four pages printed once a month. The headlines were things like "New Chicks Arrive at the General Store," or "Turo's Cousin Comes for a Visit." In fact, it seemed like they *needed* things to write about. But Maricela was acting as if she'd been interviewed by the *New York Evening Post*.

"I guess they think I'm important, being the harvest princess *and* the daughter of the mayor."

"Wow," Pru mumbled. "Can I have your autograph?"

Maricela narrowed her eyes. "You're jealous," she told Pru.

"Am not."

"Are too. You've *always* been jealous of me."

Pru scrambled to her feet and faced Maricela with a look of defiance. "For your information, Maricela, I have *never* been jealous of you."

"Oh really?" Maricela smiled smugly. "Even when I got the lead in the play? Even when my speech was chosen for Founder's Day?"

Pru's expression fell.

"Some people are winners and some people are losers," Maricela said in her singsong way. "And you're a loser. A *sore* loser."

Pru's face tightened into a scowl. Her arms went stiff and she balled up her fists. Abigail scrambled to her feet and darted in front of Pru. "Hey, Maricela, would you like a piece of cake?" Abigail asked pleasantly, clearly trying to lighten the situation.

Maricela flicked her long auburn hair over her shoulder. "I should think not. Too much sugar is bad for you. It gives you pimples."

"Yeah, well, I'd rather have pimples than be covered in stinkbugs." Pru pointed to Maricela's shoulder, where a green stinkbug was crawling. Maricela squealed and flicked the bug away. Then Pru pointed to another that was on her sleeve. Maricela squealed again.

Where were those bugs coming from? Lucky's gaze traveled to the top of Maricela's head. "They like your flowers," she said, pointing to the crown.

"Or maybe they like *you*," Pru told Maricela. "I sure hope they don't *crawl into your ears*."

Maricela tore the crown off her head and dropped it to the ground. "Stinkbugs do not like me! That's a mean thing to say." Then, with a quick turn on her heel, she marched away. Pru snickered.

"What's the deal with you two?" Lucky asked.

"We don't get along," Pru said. "It's always been this way."

"You shouldn't let her get you so worked up," Abigail said, gently placing her hand on Pru's arm.

Pru sighed. "I know. But she gets under my skin like a bug bite."

Lucky couldn't blame Pru for getting annoyed. Maricela was definitely a difficult personality. But Lucky suspected that Pru wasn't being totally honest. Something had happened. Something was not being said.

A bell clanged. Abigail clapped her hands. "Yay," she cried out. "It's time!"

"Time for what?" Lucky asked.

Pru's mood immediately lightened. "It's the best part of the festival."

Abigail grabbed Lucky's hand. "Come on!"

4

Everyone hurried toward the clanging bell, like cattle to a feeding trough. The air buzzed with excitement. Wide-eyed kids raced to get there first. "Gather 'round, gather 'round," Mayor Gutierrez called from the steps of Town Hall. "The time has come!"

"What's going on?" Lucky asked, but Abigail merely gave her a mischievous smile. Lucky looked to Pru, but Pru offered no clues.

"You'll see," she said mysteriously.

Lucky had no idea what to expect. She forgot all about her tummyache as Abigail led her into the crowd.

"Let me through. I'm little!" Snips hollered as he jabbed with his elbows. "I wanna see!" Abigail cleverly followed in her brother's wake, as did Lucky and Pru, until they found a prime spot at the front of the crowd.

Lucky looked around. Once again, the mayor stood on a stool, waving his arms for attention. Maricela and Mrs. Gutierrez were at his side. Maricela fidgeted and scratched her neck, then checked her sleeves for more bugs. Her mother told her to stop fidgeting. A wagon was parked in front of the town hall steps. A wooden crate sat inside. Lucky flared her nostrils. A weird scent hung in the air.

A farmer stood next to the wagon. Lucky had seen the man before, but she didn't know his name. He lived on the outskirts of town. He looked like most of Miradero's farmers, his skin leathered from working in the sun. He wore a wide-brimmed hat and a flannel shirt. A pair of work gloves were tucked into the back pocket of his jeans.

"Ladies and gentlemen, citizens of Miradero, welcome to the closing ceremony of our harvest festival," Mayor Gutierrez said. "I hope you all had fun today." People clapped and cheered. Snips could barely contain himself, jumping up and down. He rushed forward and tried to peer into the crate.

"Is he in there?" Snips asked. "Is he?"

The farmer blocked Snips's view. "Hold on there, young feller. You don't want to upset Mel, do ya? He's particularly sensitive."

"Sorry," Abigail said as she pulled Snips away from the wagon.

Who's Mel? Lucky thought. The breeze shifted direction. *And what's that awful stink?* She glanced across the way and made eye contact with her dad. He shrugged, as confused as she. Cora held her third-place ribbon in one hand and daintily plugged her nose with the other.

The mayor continued. "Shall we begin?" The crowd applauded again. With a grand sweep of her arm, Maricela handed her father a rolled parchment, which he unrolled and read. "Hear ye, hear ye," he began. "Let it be known that on this day, the thirtieth of October, as summer fades into memory and the autumnal season is upon us, the people of Miradero gathered together to ask Miradero Mel a question of the utmost importance: Will winter be sweet or will winter be severe?" He lowered the scroll and looked at the crate. "What say ye, Miradero Mel?"

Everyone looked at the crate. Silence fell over the crowd. Lucky chewed on her lip. What was happening? Was something happening?

Nothing was happening.

The mayor raised his voice. "What say ye, Miradero Mel?"

Lucky couldn't take another moment of not knowing. She felt like she was going to jump right out of her skin.

She leaned over and whispered in Snips's ear. "Who is Miradero Mel?"

"He's the pig!" Snips loudly proclaimed. Those around him responded with shushing sounds.

A pig? That explained the odor. Lucky stood on tiptoe, trying to see into the crate. What was the pig supposed to do?

For a few more moments, nothing kept right on happening. Finally, the farmer stepped up to the wagon and rapped his knuckles on the top of the wooden crate. A few grunts sounded from inside. Lucky leaned forward, as did everyone else. A pink snout appeared. Then a pink face with a pair of small black eyes. Snips giggled. The pig looked around, then backed up, disappearing again.

The farmer stuck a finger in the air. "He ain't comin' out!"

People began to murmur. "Uh-oh," Abigail said.

"What's going on?" Lucky pleaded.

Pru took pity on her. "It's this weird tradition. I don't know when it started, but pigs are supposed to be really smart. If the pig comes out of his house, it means winter is going to be mellow. But if the pig doesn't come out, it means winter is going to be bad."

Lucky snorted. "A pig can't predict the weather."

"He's never wrong," Abigail said matter-of-factly. "I win cakewalks and Miradero Mel predicts the weather. Some things can't be explained."

Mayor Gutierrez held up his hands to silence the crowd. "The pig has spoken. Let it be known that on this day, Miradero Mel did not come out of his house. Therefore, he has decreed that winter will be…severe." The mayor then walked into the crowd and began shaking everyone's hand. "Remember that a vote for me is a vote for progress."

Severe? Lucky frowned. That seemed overly dramatic. Miradero had been hot all summer, and now, in the middle of autumn, the days were still pleasant and mild. Even when it rained, the clouds only hung around for a short time. The only coolness to be felt was in the evenings. Back in the city, there'd be snowstorms with snow piled up three steps high. People had to shovel snow off their stoops. Traffic stopped until the roads were cleared. *These folk don't know what a real winter is*, Lucky thought.

Seriously, how bad could it get?

5

A few weeks passed and on a Sunday afternoon, the PALs went for a ride to Carver's Woods. Lucky and Spirit led the way, with Pru on her trusty mare, Chica Linda, and Abigail on her goofy but loveable Boomerang. A little cluster of rain clouds had passed through that morning, dampening the ground and filling the air with the scent of wet dirt. The distant mountains were delicately sprinkled with snow, like powdered sugar on cake. Lucky was surprised to see the snow, but it was too far away to worry about. A new chill hung in the air. She wondered if she'd soon need a heavier coat.

The girls rode a familiar trail, as they'd promised their parents. This promise was due to the near disaster a few months back, when Pru and Abigail had ridden into Filbert Canyon, unaware that railroad workers had laid dynamite. Spirit and Lucky had ridden after the girls to warn them. But they'd all ended up nearly crushed by falling rocks. Thanks to Spirit's instincts and guidance, they had found their way to safety. And now the girls were supposed to stay in approved areas only.

"I hate this new rule," Pru complained as she rode behind Lucky. "How long are they going to hold that whole dynamite thing over our heads? We survived, didn't we?"

"It doesn't bother me," Abigail said. "I don't like those steep trails in the canyon. And Boomerang doesn't like them, either."

"I'm just happy to be riding," Lucky said. She hadn't purposely taken the lead, but Spirit had. She guessed it was because he was used to leading his herd. Chica Linda and Boomerang didn't seem to mind.

She glanced back over her shoulder. Chica Linda held her head high, observing the surroundings. A palomino, her golden coat and white mane looked very pretty beneath the autumn sky. Boomerang, however, was looking down, searching for food. A brown-and-white pinto, he was the smallest of the three horses, and the plumpest. Pru often called him a "walking stomach."

"Aw, come on, Boomerang. Do you have to eat everything?" Abigail complained. Spirit and Chica Linda slowed, allowing Boomerang to catch up.

Like Pru, Chica Linda took riding seriously. And if there was a race, she'd do her best to win. Like Abigail,

Boomerang didn't much care about winning. He was just happy to be outside. He was the happiest horse Lucky had ever met.

Lucky remembered a conversation she'd once had with her aunt Cora, about how people often chose dogs that matched their personalities. Their neighbors, back in Philadelphia, were excellent examples. Mr. Bunyon, a stout, jowly man who grunted his dissatisfaction, chose a bulldog. Mrs. Tolstoy, who kept her hair in tight ringlets and spoke in a high-pitched voice, chose a pampered, yappy poodle as her companion.

It seemed to be the same with people and their horses. Boomerang was as sweet as Abigail. And Chica Linda was as competitive as Pru.

But what of Lucky and Spirit? She hadn't chosen him, and he didn't belong to her. They'd found each other quite by accident. But in ways she was still discovering, they were similar—most especially in their desire to run free.

"Let's gallop!" Pru called, as if reading Lucky's mind. With a gentle kick, she urged Chica Linda forward. The palomino flared her nostrils and bolted ahead of Spirit. Pru's braid bounced and she let out a loud "Whoopee! First one to the boulder wins!"

"Oh no you don't," Lucky said. She didn't need to kick Spirit. He paused a moment for Lucky to tighten her grip, and then he was off. Soon, he and Chica Linda were racing side by side. Pine trees flew past as the horses dodged branches and rocks. Lucky held tight, her smile so wide she actually swallowed a bug. *"Bleck!"*

Lucky had become a skilled rider in a very short time, thanks to lessons from Pru. But mostly, thanks to Spirit. It was unusual for a wild horse to allow a rider. If he wanted, he could buck her off at any time, as he had with Al Granger and the ranch hands who'd tried to break him. He'd tossed those grown men across the corral as easily as a child tosses a ball. But the thing was, not only did Spirit allow Lucky to ride him, he helped her by slowing down if she started to lose her balance. And if she leaned in the wrong direction and started losing her grip, he would adjust his stride. Not only was Spirit patient with Lucky, he seemed to enjoy their rides as much as she enjoyed them. How could she know this? Well, he kept coming back for more!

Pru had pointed out that one of the reasons Lucky had learned so quickly was because she rode bareback. "Without a saddle, you're forced to rely on your balance or you'll slide right off. It's kinda like do or die," Pru had told her. *Bareback* meant that Lucky had nothing to hold on to but Spirit's mane, and it also meant she could feel his every move. So they'd learned how to read each other's body language. They'd learned to move together. It was true teamwork, requiring grace and skill.

There were others in town who didn't understand why Lucky would want to ride bareback. "It's much more comfortable in a saddle," Al Granger had argued. But Lucky refused to stick a saddle on Spirit. It went against his nature. And, as it turned out, it went against her nature, too. When she rode her dad's horse, or one of Mr. Granger's horses, the saddle and reins felt weird, like a person who writes with her right hand and is suddenly told she must write with her left.

A jackrabbit hopped across the path. Chica Linda slowed for a moment, then both horses skidded to a stop at the base of the boulder. "Tie!" Lucky called.

"Yeah, yeah, but one of these days..." Pru's face was flushed from the ride. She eased Chica Linda toward a stream for a drink. "One of these days she'll beat Spirit."

"Maybe," Lucky said. "If Spirit *lets* her."

It was good-natured ribbing. Both girls knew that Spirit was probably the strongest horse they'd ever meet. As he dipped his head to drink, Lucky turned around to check on Abigail. She and Boomerang were taking their time, enjoying the trail. Lucky nudged Spirit closer to Chica Linda. "Pru?"

"Yeah?" Pru pulled two pieces of jerky from her pocket. She handed one to Lucky.

"Thanks." Lucky didn't eat right away. Something was bugging her. If there was one thing Lucky Prescott did not like, it was an unanswered question. "So, Pru…at the harvest festival…"

"Uh-huh." Pru tore a piece of jerky with her teeth.

Lucky hesitated. Was she being too nosy? But she remembered the expression on Pru's face when Maricela had called her a loser. "Why are things so bad between you and Maricela?"

Pru's eyes narrowed. She chewed, then swallowed. "It's not important. Just let it go." Pru's tone was a warning, like a DO NOT TRESPASS sign.

Lucky suddenly felt bad. She had overstepped. Even though it felt as if they'd been friends their whole lives, it had actually been only a few months. Pru had a secret and she didn't want to share it. Lucky would have to accept that and respect Pru's privacy.

But still, the question clung to her thoughts like a stinkbug.

Pru smiled at Lucky, letting her know things were okay between them. A loud group of ravens landed on the boulder and started fighting over the remains of a snake. As Spirit and Chica Linda turned away from the stream, their thirsts quenched, Abigail and Boomerang rode up. Abigail's nose was pink, as were her cheeks. "It's getting cold out here," she said.

"Sure is." Lucky shivered as a chilly breeze tickled the back of her neck. After waiting for Boomerang to take a drink, the PALs turned back toward town.

"Dad says we need to get the barn ready for winter," Pru told them. "There are some holes that need to be repaired before the snow comes."

"Snow?" Lucky asked.

"Miradero Mel said winter's going to be severe, so that means snow. Lots and lots of snow."

"The last time we got a lot of snow was when we were little," Abigail said. "But I remember how much fun it was. The pond froze over and Mom took me ice-skating."

"And we made snowmen," Pru said.

"Snow *ladies*," Abigail reminded her with a chuckle.

Pru laughed. "Oh, that's right. But that was so long ago I'd almost forgot."

Lucky pulled her jacket collar up around her neck. "Back in the city it snows every winter."

"Every winter?" Abigail asked. "You're so lucky. Ha ha, get it? So lucky?" Abigail accepted a piece of jerky from Pru. "What did you do when it snowed?"

"Well, we'd make snowmen—and snow ladies—too. And I loved starting snowball fights! But we'd usually get yelled at by our headmistress, Madame Barrow, if she saw us. And then we'd have to stay inside."

"Well, I'm not staying inside if it snows," Pru declared. "No way!"

Lucky placed her hand on Spirit's neck, absorbing the warmth. "What will Spirit's herd do if it snows?" she asked. "Won't they freeze?"

"Oh, I wouldn't worry about them," Abigail said. "Look at Spirit. He's already growing his winter coat. They all are." It was true that the three horses looked shaggier than usual, but Spirit was definitely shaggier than Boomerang or Chica Linda. Lucky figured it was because those two horses had a barn to stay in when it got cold and had no need to worry about freezing on the open range.

Lucky ruffled Spirit's coat. "Maybe this will keep him warm, but what will the mustangs eat if everything gets covered in snow?"

Before Pru or Abigail could answer, a whistle sounded. They'd emerged from Carver's Woods just as a puff of smoke appeared on the horizon. Forgetting all about her unanswered question, Lucky sat up straight. "It's here!" she said. The arrival of the train meant one thing for Lucky—one very important thing. She grabbed Spirit's mane. "Come on!"

6

Miradero's train station was nothing like the one
back in Philadelphia, which was always crowded with
travelers and vendors, with multiple trains arriving and
departing every day. But in Miradero, the train only
made its appearance a few times a month. It wasn't
unusual for the townsfolk to stop whatever they were
doing and hurry toward the station, just to see who was
disembarking.

While Pru and Abigail waited outside the station
with the horses, Lucky made her way through the station
house and out onto the platform. Steam swirled like
mist from a fairy tale as the large black engine arrived.
Sputtering and hissing sounded as the train came to a
stop. The conductor stepped out, took off his hat, and
nodded at Lucky. A few people disembarked and were
greeted with hugs by family. But Lucky was looking for
one person in particular.

"Samuel!" she called with a wave.

"Hello, Lucky." Samuel, the stationmaster, was an
easygoing, friendly man who insisted that everyone call

him by his first name. He wore a pair of overalls and a plaid shirt with the sleeves rolled up. "You looking for anything in particular?" he teased, knowing full well why she was there. She nodded.

Lucky followed Samuel to the first car. He opened the door, reached in, and grabbed a large mail pouch, which he handed to Lucky. Then he grabbed two more pouches. They carried them into the stationhouse. "Go ahead," he told her while he helped some passengers with their luggage. Lucky shuffled through the first pouch until she found a small package wrapped in brown paper and tied with twine. "For Miss Lucky Prescott, care of JP & Sons Railroad Office, Miradero," she whispered, snatching it like a hungry squirrel snatches a peanut. "Thank you," she called to Samuel, then ran outside.

"Is it from Emma?" Abigail asked.

"Yes."

Abigail reached into her saddlebag and took out one of her famous oatmeal cookies. She broke it into three pieces and fed a piece to each horse as a little treat. Then, while the horses lowered their heads and grazed, the girls sat on a bench with Lucky in the middle.

Emma Popham was Lucky's best friend back in the

city. They'd been schoolmates, and she was Lucky's main connection to her old life. Lucky's grandfather, James Sr., still lived in Philadelphia, but letters from Emma were much more exciting. Emma and Lucky shared secrets, hopes, and dreams. And Emma also sent packages—books, to be exact. Lucky untied the twine. A note was tucked underneath.

Dear Lucky,

I was at the bookstore and I found the latest Boxcar Bonnie book and guess what? It's about a horse! So, of course, I knew you'd want to read it.

There's not much new here. Madame Barrow still doesn't approve of my reading choices. She says that if I read too many adventure stories, I will develop an overactive imagination and that will lead to trouble. She gave me a copy of her new book, How to Make Polite Conversation. It's sooooo boring.

My dad bought a new carriage horse last week. He's a palomino, like Chica Linda. I named him Captain Nemo. He's a bit temperamental but I think that's because he doesn't know us yet. I'm bringing him lots of treats and he's starting to trust me. He goes crazy for carrots.

I miss you so much. Can't wait to get your next letter and hear about all your adventures.

Love,
Emma

P.S. My parents promise that I can come visit you in the spring. I'm so happy! I'll get to meet Pru and Abigail. And Spirit!

"She's gonna visit?" Pru asked. "That's great. I can't wait to meet her."

Emma's upcoming visit was the best news ever. Lucky opened the paper wrapping and held up the slim novel. She read its title. *"Boxcar Bonnie and the Missing Mustang."*

"Missing mustang?" Abigail frowned. "Can you imagine if one of our horses went missing?" They each glanced across the way, to the cluster of juniper trees where Chica Linda, Boomerang, and Spirit continued to graze. Lucky didn't want to imagine such a thing. If something ever happened to Spirit...

She shook the thought from her head. "I'm sure the book has a happy ending," she said. "They always do."

"Girls!" Samuel stood in front of the station, a broom in hand. "Would you be able to do me a favor?"

Pru jumped to her feet. "Sure thing. What do you need?"

"Mary Pat and Bianca are both home with the sniffles. They usually take the mail into town for me." Mary Pat and Bianca were Samuel's twin daughters. Even though they were only six years old, they were quite independent and could often be found riding tandem on their horse, Tugaboo.

"Sure, we can do it!" Abigail said.

After Lucky, Pru, and Abigail had mounted their horses, Samuel handed each a mail pouch, which they draped across their horses' shoulders. Then, with a good-bye wave, they headed into town.

But just as they reached the bend in the road, Spirit stopped. He turned toward the mountains, his ears alert. "Spirit, what's wrong?" Lucky asked.

"Look, it's his herd," Pru said.

A few mustangs appeared on the horizon. They also stopped, keeping their distance. Spirit stomped his front hoof. Then he whinnied. A faint whinny was returned.

"What's wrong?" Lucky pleaded. He whinnied again, then began to shuffle back and forth. "Okay, okay, I'll get off," she said. She grabbed the mail pouch and slid to the ground. The result was immediate. Spirit took off, charging toward his herd.

"Uh, well, good-bye to you, too!" Lucky called, feeling a bit neglected.

"I wouldn't worry about it," Pru told her. "He's a free spirit."

Lucky wrapped her arms around the heavy mail bag, watching as Spirit raced away. It was odd for him to leave without a good-bye snort.

Was something wrong?

7

Cora Prescott opened the door to the Miradero
general store and stepped inside. A little bell jingled
overhead, announcing her arrival.

"Howdy, Miss Cora. I'll be with you just as soon as I
finish helping Orval." The voice belonged to Winthrop,
the store's owner.

Cora nodded and grabbed a basket. This week's
shopping list was longer than usual. She headed toward
the clothing section. Jim had been spending so much
time on his feet overseeing the railroad workers that he
was wearing right through his socks. Three new pairs
would do nicely. And Lucky had lost another hair ribbon
during a ride, so that needed to be replaced.

In Cora's former life, her housekeeper had done all
the shopping. And cooking. And cleaning. But this was
her new life, and she was surprised to discover that
she didn't mind the work. Back in Philadelphia, Cora
had overseen fund raising efforts for libraries and art
museums, and the results could be measured in large
ways. But here, cooking a meal or buying a sock, the

results were measured by the gratitude of her family. By love. She felt needed in a whole new way.

The wooden floorboards creaked beneath her boots as she perused the ribbon selection. The general store was a cluttered place, carrying most everything a family needed—brooms, dish towels, frying pans, and kettles to name a few. There were department store catalogs for ordering special items.

A fat white cat wound around Cora's feet. Cora had never been one to keep pets. But last month a rogue field mouse had chewed a hole through her sugar bag. She now understood the sensibleness of keeping a cat.

As she reached down to pet the purring creature, the conversation between Winthrop and Orval caught her attention. "I'm gonna have to double my order," Orval said. "On account of the weather. Don't want to go hungry like those other folks. They nearly starved to death."

Cora's spine stiffened. "Starved to death?" she asked. The two men turned and looked at her.

Winthrop was quite young to be a business owner, but that wasn't unusual in the West, where opportunity existed if you were willing to take a chance and set out on your own, often without family or friends. His customer, Mr. Orval Sanchez, was a goat farmer.

Orval pulled a toothpick from his mouth. "Don't mean to worry you, ma'am. But Miradero Mel says we got severe weather coming in."

"Miradero Mel?" Cora stepped over the cat and approached the misguided farmer. "Mr. Sanchez," she said with a pitiful look, "surely you can't be serious about listening to a pig."

"As serious as a tortoise on a fence post," he said, pushing his ten-gallon hat up his forehead.

Winthrop smacked his hand on the counter. "I never heard that one before." He laughed. "A tortoise on a fence post. I'm gonna have to remember that one."

Cora loosened her wool scarf. The general store's stove was putting out some heat. "There is a difference between folklore and fact," she insisted. "A pig cannot predict weather."

Mr. Sanchez and Winthrop shared a look of confusion. "You don't believe the pig?" Mr. Sanchez asked.

"I'm sure it's a very nice pig, but really, it's a...*pig*."

Winthrop moved down the counter, past the display of beeswax candles and the basket of lemon-scented soap, until he stood directly across from Cora. "Miss Prescott," he said, in a very serious voice, "I know you're new to these parts, so our customs may sound a bit strange to you. But that pig is so smart, he could go and get himself a university degree."

Mr. Sanchez nodded. "If Mel says it's gonna be bad, then it's gonna be bad. Real bad."

"Badder than it's ever been," Winthrop said, lowering his voice to an eerie whisper.

Cora pursed her lips. She wasn't going to let some folktale scare her. How silly these people were with their superstitions. She held out her list. "I need eggs," she said. "And flour. And sugar."

The front door opened and the bell jingled again. Lucky, Pru, and Abigail charged in, panting and stumbling as they each carried a large mail pouch. A display of jam jars rattled. Winthrop's eyes went wide. "You kids be careful. You might break something!"

"We brought the mail," Lucky told him. With a thud, her pouch landed on the floor, as did Pru's and Abigail's.

Since coming to Miradero, Cora often found herself

looking at Lucky as if she hadn't seen her in months. Was that girl in the pants and cowboy boots really her niece? Cora had always recognized the wildness that flowed through Lucky, an energy she'd inherited from her mother. But now, in Miradero, that energy was more obvious, no longer stifled by starched collars or long wool skirts.

"Hi, Aunt Cora." Lucky's cheeks were pink, her eyes sparkling. The outdoors suited her.

"Hello, Lucky." Cora kissed her cheek. "Hello, Pru and Abigail."

"Hello, Miss Prescott," the girls replied. Cora was so pleased that Lucky had made friends. Both Pru and Abigail were delightful young ladies with excellent manners. Cora highly approved.

While Winthrop lugged the pouches behind the counter, Abigail sank to the floor and pulled the white cat into her arms. "You're so fluffy!" She pressed her face against the back of the cat's neck.

Lucky glanced at the list in Cora's hand. "You need help?"

"That would be nice," Cora told her.

Pru stepped up to the counter. "Hey, Winthrop," she

said. "My dad wanted me to tell you that we'll need to order extra oats for the horses."

"You and everyone else," he grumbled. "A bad winter is going to be good for business, but it sure means a lot more work."

Cora put a jar of mustard into her basket. "Pru? Does your father believe that winter is going to be severe?"

"He sure does," Pru replied.

This surprised Cora. Al Granger seemed an intelligent man. Why would he fall for such a silly tale?

"Pigs are smart," Abigail said as she continued to sit on the floor and pet the cat.

"Animals can sense things that people can't sense," Pru said. "My mom wrote a paper about it." Pru's mother, Fanny Granger, was the town's only veterinarian. "If you go outside and look around, you'll see that the snakes have disappeared into their holes earlier this year. And the songbirds have migrated earlier, too. And just look at the wild horse herd. We've never seen their coats so shaggy. All those things point to a cold winter."

Mr. Sanchez settled onto one of the counter stools. He took out a pouch of tobacco and began to fill his pipe. "I remember the old-timers talking 'bout the first winter. They called it 'the winter of the starving.'"

Both Pru and Lucky gasped. Abigail stopped petting the cat and got to her feet. "I've never heard that story," Pru said.

"What happened?" Lucky asked. Even Cora couldn't hide her curiosity. She set her shopping basket on the counter, then sat on another stool, ready to absorb the tale.

Mr. Sanchez tapped his pipe to settle the tobacco. Then he looked up at his audience. "Well, back in the old days, Miradero wasn't a town. It was just a couple of shacks where the railroad workers lived. And after a couple of months, their families joined them. But there was no general store. They didn't have anything but those shacks. All their food and supplies came by wagon, and what they didn't get, they had to hunt and gather themselves."

Cora tried to imagine living in such an isolated way. It was difficult enough that there was only one type of black tea at Winthrop's General Store, but at least there was tea!

Mr. Sanchez continued. "But that first winter was harsh. The snow was so high they could hardly open the doors. They huddled together in the shacks. They melted snow for drinkin', but as the weeks passed, the wagons couldn't reach them on account of the blizzards and avalanches. So they ran out of food."

"What happened to them?" Abigail asked, the white cat hanging from her arms.

"One day, a group of *mesteñeros* was riding through. They'd come looking for mustangs. The *mesteñeros* heard an eerie sound. They thought it was the wind, but as they got closer, they discovered it was people crying for help." Cora shuddered. She reached out and pulled Lucky close. "They dug through the snow and opened the first shack's door. They found the families in a real pitiful state, as skinny as string beans. The *mesteñeros* fed them."

"Whew!" Abigail cried. The cat scampered away.

"The *mesteñeros* ended up staying. They stayed for the rest of their lives and helped build the town."

"So no one died?" Lucky asked.

Mr. Sanchez shook his head. "Not that I know of. But they came real close."

"Well, that wouldn't happen now," Cora insisted. "Even if winter is severe, we have the railroad to bring our supplies."

"Don't be so sure," Winthrop said. "Even a train can be stopped by the weather. Nature is mighty powerful."

Mr. Sanchez pointed his pipe at Cora. "That's why I say, listen to the pig! Don't get stuck like a tortoise on a fence post. Ready yourself for the bad weather, or else you could starve."

An eerie feeling washed over Cora. This time she did not argue.

8

A fire flickered in the hearth, casting warmth and
light throughout the parlor. Evening had set. Jim lit the
parlor's lanterns. He also pulled the heavy curtains, to
keep out the chilly night air, which had a way of seeping
through the windows. Lucky sat on the carpet. She'd set
her homework on the coffee table. She had a whole page
of math problems due tomorrow, but no matter how hard
she tried to focus, her mind was elsewhere.

Why had Spirit run off? It was so unusual for him to
do so. Maybe Pru was right, that he'd simply wanted to
join his herd and play. Was Lucky being silly? Spirit was
a horse, after all, not a person who'd been taught that it
was good manners to say hello and good-bye. She smiled
to herself. Yes, he'd just been acting like a horse. But still,
he usually said good-bye in his own way, with a nudge or
a snort.

"This cake is scrumptious."

That exuberant voice snapped Lucky out of her
thoughts. Althea Bradley, owner of the town's only inn,
had stopped by for a visit. Althea was the president of
the Miradero Ladies' Aid Society; Cora was the treasurer.

And it just so happened that Jim had taken a pound cake out of the oven a few minutes before her arrival.

"Glad you like it," Jim told her. "Cora's teaching me some of the basics. Gotta do my share around here." He sat in his favorite chair, his long legs stretched out, his slipper-covered feet resting on an ottoman. There were no formalities when Althea visited. She often said, "Don't need anything fancy. I'm as happy as a pig in a puddle." She had a colorful way of speaking, and a colorful way of living. While she and Cora had become very close friends, they were quite different. If they were bouquets of flowers, Cora would be perfectly arranged, with delicate hues and trimmed stems—flowers that had been grown carefully in a garden. Althea, on the other hand, would be a bunch of wild flowers, vibrant colors tied together with twine— flowers that had survived in difficult places; still lovely, though, weeds and all.

"If you try real hard, you might convince me to have a second helping." Althea's eyes sparkled. She held out her plate.

"Please, have as much as you'd like," Cora said, cutting another piece.

"Well, if you insist!"

Althea settled against a pillow to enjoy her cake. Her blond hair was tied back in a ponytail. Her brown dress had fringe on the sleeves and her leather belt matched her leather boots. She was a rather plump woman, and tonight her face was pinkish on account of her sitting close to the fire. "Mighty fine cake."

Lucky put down her pencil. "Althea, how long have you lived here?"

"All my life, young lady. I'm like that old walnut tree, the one next to the church. There's no moving us. Our roots go deep." She laughed, then took another bite.

"Do you know the story about the first winter in Miradero?"

Althea stopped eating. "My great-granddad lived through that winter. He got so hungry, he nearly ate his own foot!"

Cora cringed.

"You don't say," Jim said. "His own foot?"

Althea nodded. "They got so hungry, they ate tree bark, like animals."

Lucky tried to imagine such a scene. She'd felt hungry after coming home late for supper once in a while. But she couldn't imagine eating tree bark. Cora filled a teacup with black tea and set it in front of Althea.

"Now, now, Althea, you'll give Lucky nightmares. Jim, tell Lucky not to worry. The train will always bring us food and supplies."

"We'll, I'd like to say that's the case, but..." Jim set his cup aside. "The train is a machine, Cora. It's not infallible. Weather can be a serious factor. Blizzards. Avalanches. Those sorts of things can stop a train."

Cora's brow creased. "Oh, now I'm worried," she said. "What happens if winter is as bad as everyone believes? What happens if we run out of supplies?"

"I'm not eating my own foot," Lucky said.

"And you're not eating mine!" Althea winked at her.

Cora rose from the couch and began pacing. "I don't know how to prepare for winter. Al Granger is ordering extra feed for his horses. But what about us? Should I be storing extra food? What should I be doing?"

Althea reached out and took Cora's hand, pulling her back to the couch. "Settle down, Cora. No use getting your nerves all in a tangle." She pushed aside her empty plate. "I think we should discuss this at tomorrow's meeting of the society. Information is power! If we share ideas and tips, we can help one another get ready. We can make sure each household has enough candles, firewood, and canned food. And most especially, we need to think about the elderly, the ones who live alone with no one to look after them."

"There's old Mrs. Marsh," Lucky pointed out.

"There sure is," Althea said. "And old Mr. Broomgerry. He lives all alone up there in the hills. His legs aren't so good anymore. We'll need to make sure they have enough blankets and lantern oil and such."

"This is an excellent idea," Jim said.

"Growing old alone is not for the faint of heart." Althea gave Jim a long look. "You wouldn't be fixin' on growing old *alone*, would you, Jim?"

Jim laughed. "Of course not. I have Cora and Lucky."

Althea leaned forward. "What I mean is…you ever think of getting married again?"

Lucky shifted position. What kind of question was that?

"Why, Althea, are you proposing to me?" Jim asked seriously.

Lucky froze. Was Althea proposing to her father? Did Althea *like* Jim? Silence descended—awkward, weird silence. Lucky wanted to move her legs since they were falling asleep, but she didn't want to miss a second of this exchange. Even Cora was sitting at the edge of the couch, waiting.

Then both Jim and Althea broke the silence with

laughter. Even Lucky laughed. Jim and Althea married? What a silly idea. "No, I'm not looking for a husband," Althea said. Her laughter abruptly stopped and she raised an eyebrow. "But my sister is. She lives in Boston but she'd move anywhere for a nice man."

"I'll keep your sister in mind," Jim said.

"You'd be quite the catch, Jim. Quite the catch."

Lucky half-smiled. They were still teasing each other. That was all it was. Teasing.

Althea stood. "It's getting late. I'd best skedaddle." Jim got up and collected her coat. "See you at tomorrow's meeting," she told Cora. "Good-bye, Lucky."

"Good-bye."

Just as Althea was heading out the door, she reached into her coat pocket and pulled out a piece of paper, which she handed to Jim. "My sister's mailing address. Just in case." And, with a wink, she left.

Jim closed the door, then stood there for a moment, reading the address, unaware that both Lucky and Cora were staring at him. He looked up. "What?"

Cora stepped forward. "Jim, you're not actually thinking about writing to her? Are you?"

He folded the paper. "Of course not." He ruffled Lucky's hair. "I have you two. That's all I need."

That night, as Lucky lay in bed, she stared at a poster that hung on her wall. It was an advertisement for *El Circo Dos Grillos*. In the illustration, a young woman wearing a sparkly blue dress stood on a horse's back. She was Milagro, Lucky's mother, a performer known for her courageous and unparalleled stunts with her horse, Equuleus. Lucky had never really known her mom, who'd died when Lucky was only two years old. That poster had hung on Lucky's bedroom wall for as long as she could remember, and before going to sleep she always whispered, "Good-night, Mom." But since meeting Spirit, the poster had taken on a whole new meaning. Lucky now knew that while she'd inherited her mother's skin tone, brown hair, and green eyes, she'd also inherited her natural instinct for riding and relating to horses.

Her thoughts once again turned to Spirit, hoping she'd see him tomorrow. Then she picked up her new novel, *Boxcar Bonnie and the Missing Mustang*, and began to read. But something else was bugging her, something keeping her thoughts from focusing on the page. What was it? She glanced up at Milagro. Her beloved mother. The only mother she'd ever had and ever wanted to have.

And that's when it hit her.

Even though her father had said he wasn't going to write to Althea's sister, he hadn't thrown the address away.

He'd stuck it into his pocket.

Part Two

9

Spirit and his herd approached the river, then followed an offshoot to a small pool where the water was calm and deep. They'd woken at first light and had begun the day's trek earlier than usual, knowing they'd have to cover more ground to fill their bellies. The trees were bare now, the grasses sparse.

He looked behind, in the direction where Lucky lived. Should he go see her? The herd would be fine on its own. The other mustangs were used to him going and coming, even when he returned smelling of people. Even when he carried the frightening scent of fire and the scent of other horses, the ones who never roamed free.

The herd seemed to understand Spirit's constant movement between his two worlds.

Spirit dipped his head to drink from the pool. Despite the cold weather, the mustangs were doing well. Both the colt and filly had weaned weeks ago. The colt looked healthy and strong. He chased a quail until it disappeared into a rock pile. He bucked playfully, as the young do, unaware of the coming cold and all the troubles it would bring.

But the filly caught Spirit's attention. At first, she didn't drink from the pool. Her mother nuzzled her, then gave her a push on the rump, moving her closer to the water's edge. Still, the filly didn't drink. The mother pushed her again, then nickered, urging her baby to drink. Finally, the filly lowered her head and drank. Spirit watched with curiosity. It was normal for a young horse to be distracted by the world around it, but the filly was not playing, not chasing or exploring. The mare, who happened to be Spirit's sister, cast a worried look at him. Spirit sensed the same thing his sister did.

Something was wrong.

10

Pru Granger loved mornings in her family's
kitchen. The Granger ranch house was a sprawling place,
built from massive pine trees that had been logged from
Carver's Woods. The kitchen, the center of all activity,
was the largest room. A grand table stood smack-dab
in the middle, long enough to fit Pru's family and all
the ranch hands. Because it was a working ranch, the
Grangers employed many people, including a cook
named Jacques Chance, who'd come all the way from
France to work on the railroad, but many years had
passed and he was now too old for that sort of manual
labor, so the Grangers had hired him. He'd told Pru that
his last name meant "luck" in French. Now Pru knew two
people named "Lucky."

Jacques was an amazing cook. With the Grangers'
help, he learned all the traditional western foods, such as
pancakes, fried eggs, and corn-bread hash. With the help
of Juan, one of the ranch hands, he learned how to make
traditional Mexican foods, like refried black beans and
enchiladas. And Jacques introduced everyone to his own

traditions, like soufflé and crêpes, making every meal in the Granger home a gastronomical adventure.

Why did Pru love mornings so much? Along with the delicious food to eat, there were so many people to talk to. It was like one big extended family. Plans were made, issues were discussed, all while the skillet sizzled and cutlery clanked.

"What are your plans today?" Fanny Granger asked as she sat next to Pru.

Pru glanced up from her plate of scrambled eggs and beans and smiled at her mother. "Just the usual stuff," Pru told her. "School, then riding with Abigail and Lucky."

"On Saturday I'd like you to help us work on the barn," Al Granger said. He was seated across the table with a cloth napkin tied around his neck. "There's a whole lot of repair work needin' to be done before the snow comes." The Granger barn housed the ramada's horses, including Chica Linda. Boomerang had a guest stall there, as did Spirit, though Spirit rarely spent the night.

"Sure thing," Pru said. "I'm sure Abigail and Lucky will help."

"Gonna be a big snow," Juan said as he sprinkled powdered sugar onto a crêpe.

"If it gets as bad as we think it's going to get, there will be a lot of extra work for all of us," Fanny told everyone. "One of the most common problems in winter is that horses don't drink enough because they don't like icy water. So we'll have to carry buckets of warm water to the barn in the mornings, to melt the ice in their troughs." Being Miradero's only veterinarian, Fanny was an expert on horse health and care.

"Don't worry, Mrs. Granger, ma'am," said a farmhand named Ralph. "Boris and I can do that."

"Ralph, I'd also like you and Boris to check the barn roof," Al Granger said. "Make sure there are no weak spots or leaks."

"You got it, Mr. Granger, sir."

"*Mm, mm*, Jacques, you're one fine grub slinger," Boris said.

"These skinny pancakes are as good as cream gravy," said Ralph.

Jacques smiled, for in ranch hand lingo, that was a huge compliment. *"Merci beaucoup."*

As they finished their meal, there was more talk about the weather. And talk about ordering feed and supplies. Pru glanced at the grandfather clock. It was time to leave for school. She carried her dish to the sink and thanked Jacques for breakfast. Then she said good-bye to everyone. Lunch bag in hand, she set out for school.

Even though the schoolhouse was in walking distance, on most mornings Pru chose to ride Chica Linda. Chica Linda and Boomerang liked to hang out together in the school corral so the girls could visit with them at lunchtime. But with the weather getting colder, Pru and Abigail had agreed to leave the horses in the barn. It was the coldest morning Pru could remember, with ice crystals sparkling on the ground. Her breath drifted from her nostrils like fog. She pulled a scarf around her face.

The schoolhouse was the only school in town. It was a small red building with a coatroom and a single classroom. The wooden desks stood in tidy rows facing the teacher's desk, with the blackboard behind. When Pru arrived at school, Abigail was already at her desk. Even though the wood stove radiated heat,

Abigail still wore her hat and mittens. "Hi," Pru said, taking her seat next to Abigail. "Wow, your nose is super red."

"I almost froze out there," Abigail told her.

Snips marched up to Pru. "Did you know that if you sneeze outside, your snot freezes to your face?" He asked this question in his usual loud way.

"Thanks for the warning," Pru said with a smile. Then she looked around. "Where's Lucky?"

"Late again," Abigail said with a frown. "Miss Flores isn't going to be happy about that."

Pru looked over at Miss Flores. She was the only teacher in Miradero, and while she was very nice, she didn't like tardiness. She kept an attendance board on the wall, and at the end of the year, the students with the best attendance record got a special certificate and cupcake. Pru and Maricela were currently tied for first place.

"I'm here!" Maricela announced as she entered the classroom. Then, as if making her way across a stage, she sashayed up to Miss Flores's desk and held out a package that was tied with a red ribbon. "I brought you some chocolate-covered cherries," she said, loud enough for everyone to hear. Pru rolled her eyes. Maricela was always trying to bribe their teacher into liking her, which wasn't fair, because not everyone could afford to bring Miss Flores special presents.

"Thank you," Miss Flores said politely, setting the cherries into a drawer that was filled with Maricela's other gifts.

"You are so very welcome, Miss Flores. I thought you'd like them. They came all the way from Chicago." Without so much as a "hello" to anyone else, Maricela took her seat in the front row.

"Snips, it's your turn to ring the bell," Miss Flores said. She waited patiently as Snips *whoopee*-ed his way across the room, ran up the back stairs to the bell tower, and clanged the bell a dozen times. "Snips! That's enough!" Miss Flores called as everyone else put their fingers in their ears. "Good gracious, you only need to ring it twice."

"But I like ringing it!" he called, scampering back to his seat.

"All right, everyone," Miss Flores announced with a clap of her hands. "It's time to start our day. I will now collect your math homework."

A gust of cold air hit the back of Pru's neck. She

turned around. Lucky was standing in the doorway, one hand on the knob, the other holding her lunch bag. "Sorry I'm late," she announced, her nose as red as Abigail's.

"Oh my goodness, shut that door before we all catch pneumonia," Maricela said, as if she were in charge of everyone.

"It's so nice to know that you're worried about my health," Pru told her.

Maricela glowered at her, her voice just above a whisper. "You *should* be worried about your health. If you get sick, then you won't have a perfect attendance record and I'll win. Again." She smirked.

Pru smirked back. "Sorry to disappoint you, Maricela, but I'm as fit as a fiddle." Pru had decided that no matter what, even if she had a toothache or broke both her legs, she wouldn't let *anything* keep her from school this year. She was determined to beat Maricela at something. Maybe Maricela did have a better singing voice and that's why she got the lead in the play, and maybe she was a better speechwriter and that's why her speech was chosen for Founder's Day, but the wins were adding up and Maricela would never let her forget it.

Lucky had closed the door and was now talking to Miss Flores. Her long brown hair was messy from running, and she gasped between words as she tried to catch her breath. "I'm late because you'll never guess... what I saw," she began to explain. "There was this huge golden eagle... and it was chasing this rabbit. I thought about helping the rabbit... but then I thought, well, an eagle... needs to eat, too."

Miss Flores's expression was serious. "Lucky, it is important to be on time for class."

Pru looked over at the attendance board. Lucky had fewer stars than anyone else.

"Yes, Miss Flores," Lucky said. "I've just never seen anything... like that. We didn't have eagles in my old neighborhood."

"I appreciate your curiosity and I encourage it. But punctuality is a valuable skill to learn. And this isn't the first morning you've gotten distracted. It seems to be a pattern with you. What if you left your house earlier?"

"But I did leave early," Lucky admitted.

Maricela's hand darted into the air, as it tended to do throughout the day. Pru thought Maricela could save herself a lot of energy if she just kept that hand stuck up there all the time. She could tie a board to her arm to help keep it in the air. "Miss Flores, I could assist Lucky in getting to school on time. I could walk with her and keep her from getting distracted."

Miss Flores nodded. "I think that's an excellent idea."

"What?" Lucky's eyes widened. She glanced over at Pru and Abigail. Her expression clearly said, *Help me!*

Pru stood. "Miss Flores, I'll help Lucky get to school on time."

"Me too," Abigail said.

"I should do it," Maricela said. "I have a perfect attendance record."

"So do I," Pru told her.

Miss Flores thought for a moment. "Those are very nice offers, but Maricela did volunteer first. For the next few weeks, Maricela will escort Lucky to school." Maricela beamed. Pru lowered her eyes and sank into her chair. Well, she'd tried to help. Poor Lucky, stuck walking to school with the harvest princess.

Miss Flores motioned for Lucky to take her seat, then continued collecting homework.

"I tried," Pru grumbled as Lucky sat.

"Thanks," Lucky told her.

"Did you see Spirit this morning?" Abigail whispered.

"No. I haven't seen him in five days," Lucky whispered back. "I'm kind of worried."

"I'm sure Spirit is fine." Abigail smiled sweetly.

Miss Flores placed the worksheets on her desk, then turned to face the class. "Because Miradero Mel predicted that we are going to have a severe winter, and because the first day of winter is just around the corner, I've decided that our next group project should have a winter theme. This time, however, the groups will be based on age." She began to assign people to their groups. "Pru, Abigail, Lucky, and Maricela will work together in the twelve-year-old group."

"No way!" both Maricela and Pru said, each folding her arms tightly and turning her back to the other. "I'm not working with her!"

Miss Flores sighed. "It will be good for you two to work together."

Pru couldn't believe her ears. *Good?* Apparently she and Miss Flores had totally different definitions for the word *good*. Pru felt her face heat up. Didn't Miss Flores understand that it was impossible to work with Maricela?

Pru Granger had decided that she'd never miss a day of school no matter what, but now she was hoping that a toothache would save her from this horrid assignment.

11

Following Miss Flores's directions, Lucky, Pru, Abigail, and Maricela pushed their desks together. Then they just stared at one another, in awkward silence. Lucky could feel the tension between Pru and Maricela, the way it feels just before a wishbone snaps, but minus the excitement that a wish might come true.

"So," Lucky said, trying to approach the subject delicately. Pru and Maricela both sat with their arms tightly folded, staring at the floor. "So," she repeated. More silence. Lucky looked over her shoulder. The other groups were busy talking. Snips was teamed up with the twins, Mary Pat and Bianca, and they were huddled in a deep discussion. Even the oldest students were taking this seriously.

"Come on, you two," Abigail said with a pout. "This isn't going to be any fun if you act like this."

"Yeah, I agree. We can make this work," Lucky said, hoping that was true. "We just have to find a subject we all want to study. As team captain, I open the discussion." Miss Flores had assigned everyone a team captain. Lucky wasn't sure why she'd been chosen, but she was grateful for the opportunity to prove to Miss Flores that she was worthy.

Maricela tucked a strand of hair behind her ear. "I have straight As, so I should choose the subject."

Lucky frowned. "This is a group project. We all get a voice."

"Do any of you have straight As?" Maricela asked. When no one replied, she smirked. "Exactly. You don't. So I should choose our topic."

"No way," Pru said, sitting up straight.

"You haven't even heard my idea," Maricela told her.

"What's your idea?" Abigail asked.

Maricela swept her hands through the air, palms out, as if wiping condensation off a window. "Winter fashion," she said, with eyebrows raised. "Isn't that a great idea? We could study winter clothing styles from all over the world. And we could have a fashion show." She sat back in her chair with a look of expectation. "Everyone will love it."

Abigail's eyes lit up. "*Oooh*, that sounds…" Then she caught Pru's scowl. "Uh, Pru, what do you think?"

Pru folded her hands on her desk. "I vote we study how animals survive in the winter. My mom could help us with the research."

Maricela's upper lip curled into a sneer. "When you say *animals*, I suppose you mean *horses*."

"Well, yes, horses. But other animals, too, like the squirrels and songbirds."

"I love this idea," Lucky said. "But I'd like to add wild horses to the list. I'm really curious about what they do in the winter. We could observe Spirit's herd."

"I'm in," said Abigail, raising her hand.

"This is so predictable." Maricela was pouting now. "All you three think and talk about is horses, horses, horses."

"Oh?" Pru leaned across her desk and stuck her face real close to Maricela's. "And what do you do that's so interesting?"

Maricela began to count on her fingers. "French lessons, piano lessons, singing lessons, elocution lessons—"

"So predictable," Pru grumbled, slumping back into her seat.

"We're not agreeing on anything," Abigail said. "What should we do?"

"We live in a democracy," Pru said. "Three to one is a majority and the majority rules."

Lucky, Pru, and Abigail looked at Maricela. Lucky sensed she was not going to react well to not getting her way. And indeed, she did not.

"Miss Flores!" Maricela's hand shot up again. Her cheeks burst into color. She stomped her foot. "Miss Flores!"

Miss Flores approached their desks. "Yes, Maricela?"

"Pru, Abigail, and Lucky are ganging up on me. They aren't listening to what I want."

"And she's not listening to what we want," Pru defended.

Miss Flores stuck her pencil behind her ear, then glanced across the room to where Snips's discussion with his team had turned into a game of chase. "I'm not going to tell you girls what to do," Miss Flores said. "You must figure out a way to work together. Find something that you will all enjoy. Something you all can agree upon, or I'm afraid you won't pass." She turned sharply on her heels. "Snips!"

"Gee, how are we going to find something we all want?" Abigail asked.

"I'm not going to agree to anything that has to do with horses," Maricela informed them. "So there."

Once again, Lucky's team sat in silence. This turn of events was worrisome to Lucky. She was already in trouble thanks to her tardiness. And over the past few months she'd turned in some homework late—not out of laziness, but because there'd been so much she'd had to get used to in this new life. Chores, such as laundry, sweeping, and cooking, took a long time. She really wanted to do well on this group project. She wanted to show Miss Flores that she was a dedicated student. But if Pru and Maricela continued to act stubbornly, then they'd all fail!

Miss Flores clapped her hands. "Attention, everyone. I think you've had enough time to discuss. Now I'd like each group to tell us what they've decided to do." She pointed around the room. Snips, Mary Pat, and Bianca said they wanted to make snow cones out of real snow. Because they were only six years old, Miss Flores thought that was an appropriate choice. Turo (who was a good friend to the PALs) and the older students were going to map the winter sky. Then Miss Flores turned to Lucky's group. "We don't know yet," Lucky said. "Can we have more time to think about it?"

"Yes, but I'd like you to make a decision by Monday."

Pru was scowling something fierce. As was Maricela.

"How are we going to get them to agree?" Abigail whispered to Lucky.

Lucky whispered back, "I'm the team captain, so I'll figure it out. I moved across an entire continent and I learned how to ride a wild mustang. This will be a cinch."

But would it?

12

Saturday was spent helping Pru at the Granger barn.

From the outside it looked like an everyday sort of barn, red with white trim, and with a large sliding door and a peaked roof. But the PALs had transformed the interior, painting the stalls yellow with pretty green trim, and hanging decorative signs to mark which stalls belonged to Boomerang, Chica Linda, and Spirit. Each horse had a window to peek out of, but Spirit's stall was the only one that had a door, allowing him to come and go as he pleased. Sometimes he spent the night, sometimes he didn't. There was no pattern with him. Lucky had accepted this fact, but as she and Abigail walked to the Granger Ramada, she couldn't shake the worry over the fact that it had now been six days since she'd seen him.

And that's why she squealed with glee when she found him waiting inside the barn. "Spirit!" She wrapped her arms around his neck. He greeted her with a soft nicker.

"I knew there was nothing to worry about," Abigail said. She opened her lunch bag and took out an oatmeal cookie. Chica Linda delicately accepted her piece. Boomerang reached out with his teeth and grabbed his. Then he tried to grab the third piece. "No, Boomerang, this one's for Spirit." Spirit accepted the treat. "Horses sure love my oatmeal cookies."

"We love them, too," Pru said as she took one.

Lucky grabbed a brush and ran it down Spirit's flank. Even though she never trimmed his forelock or mane, he sure loved being brushed. His neck relaxed as he slowly set his head forward and down, exhaling a deep, fluttering breath through his nostrils.

Pru's father had left a note in the barn, next to three hammers, a jar of nails, and some boards. *For patching the holes*, the note read. After they'd brushed, watered, and fed their horses, the girls buttoned up their coats, wrapped scarves around their necks, and walked around the barn. They found three holes, each caused by rotting wood. They removed the old boards and replaced them with new ones. "What's this?" Lucky asked, peeking under a tarp.

"Oh, I forgot all about that," Pru said. "That's an old

sleigh. We used it when I was little. But we haven't had a big snow in a while, so it's been sitting there."

Images flooded Lucky's mind, of her family's annual sleigh ride through the park. Of the red sleigh, the beautiful white horse, the sound of bells jingling. She remembered sitting next to her grandfather, a wool blanket over their laps, sipping hot cocoa as they glided over the snow-covered lawn. With all these memories, a pang of homesickness struck her, as it did now and then.

"Lucky, are you okay?" Abigail asked, looking into her eyes. "You look sad all of a sudden."

"I'm okay. Just remembering winter back in Philadelphia. We took a sleigh ride every year."

"Maybe we'll get the chance to keep the tradition going," Pru said.

Abigail nodded. "I sure hope so. I'd love to ride in this again."

After patching the holes, the next chore was to clean the stalls. Not a pleasant job, but very necessary. It was important to keep the stalls tidy, not just for the horses, but to keep rats, mice, and other critters from nesting in them. They raked the soiled straw, dumped it into a wheelbarrow, and then scrubbed the floors. Lucky rolled up her sleeves and scrubbed the water trough. Pru cleaned out the food trough. When they'd finished the hard work, Abigail sat on a stool and made snowflakes from blank sheets of paper she'd torn from her notebook. Then they strung the snowflakes from the rafters. "It's like a winter wonderland," Lucky said. As the afternoon progressed, Lucky thought about bringing up the Maricela issue. They'd have to talk about the group project sooner than later, but she didn't want to spoil the mood.

As it turned out, Maricela spoiled the mood all by herself.

"It stinks in here," she announced as she barged into the barn, her wool hat pulled snugly around her face.

"If you don't like the way it smells, then you're free to leave," Pru told her as she pushed the wheelbarrow outside.

"I'm here to talk to Lucky." Maricela strode up to Lucky, who was sweeping cobwebs out of a corner. "I was wondering if you'd like to come over and have dinner with us tonight."

Lucky swept around Maricela's feet. "Thanks,

Maricela, but I'm going to be working until late. We have to get the barn ready in case we get a lot of snow."

"Can't you have the servants do this?"

Pru, who'd returned with the empty wheelbarrow, glowered. "We don't have servants, Maricela. We have employees. Besides, these are our horses and we want to take care of them." Chica Linda snorted.

"I don't know why you have to do so much horse stuff. They smell bad and they're dumb." Spirit didn't seem to like Maricela's nasty tone, because he stepped up to her and, with a bold look, neighed loudly. She squealed and backed away. "Oh, keep him away from me. He wants to bite me!"

"I don't blame him," Pru said. "You come in here and tell him that he stinks and that he's stupid."

Abigail finished hanging another snowflake and climbed down the stepladder. "If you just took the time to get to know them, you'd see that they're really sweet."

Spirit's ears were pinned forward, his tail slightly lifted. He had never bitten anyone, except the *mesteñeros* who'd tied him up with ropes and had tried to saddle him. But in that situation, he'd been protecting himself. Lucky was pretty sure he wouldn't bite Maricela, but he was staring at her with a look of pure annoyance. "Maricela," she said, stepping between them. "We need to talk about our group project. Have you thought about Pru's idea, that we study how animals survive in the winter?"

Maricela looked at Pru. Pru grabbed a shovel and began to walk past Maricela, but she tripped on something. A piece of manure landed right next to Maricela's boot. "Disgusting!" Maricela jumped away. "If you're not nicer to me, I'm never going to agree on our project!" And she stomped out the door.

Lucky and Abigail looked at Pru, who shrugged innocently. But when Lucky looked at the floor she didn't see anything that might have tripped her.

"Wow, I haven't seen Maricela that angry since that time Snips put a dead grasshopper in her sandwich," Abigail said. "She ate half of it before she realized."

Lucky followed Pru as she put away the wheelbarrow. "Pru," she said, "we don't have a choice. We have to work with her. Maybe it would be easier if we just did what she wants. The winter clothing thing is silly, but we could do it and get a good grade. And then we wouldn't have to keep fighting with her."

"No."

Lucky sighed. "I know you have this rivalry with Maricela, and I know she's not very nice, but I'm worried about my grades. I don't think Miss Flores likes me that much right now. I've been tardy and I've turned homework in late. If I fail this—"

Pru spun around. Her teeth were clenched. "I'm not letting Maricela have her way. Not this time!" She dropped the shovel, then pushed open the door and stomped outside. Chica Linda mimicked Pru's frustration by walking into her stall and turning her rump to everyone. Lucky was about to go after Pru but Abigail reached out.

"Let her be," she said. "She'll calm down."

"Abigail, what's the deal? Why do they hate each other so much?"

"They don't exactly *hate* each other. It's not *that* bad. It's just that they both love to win. And there's only one person in Miradero who beats Pru at stuff."

"But Maricela doesn't ride."

"Not riding. Other things. Like, last year there was a competition to see which student would give the speech at the Founder's Day parade. So we each had to write a speech, and the town council read them and they chose Maricela's."

"Was that because her dad is mayor?"

"Maybe," Abigail said with a shrug. "Pru wrote about how this town was founded by people who came from many different places in the world like Mexico, Spain, Africa, and England, and that's what makes Miradero such a special place. But Maricela's speech was about how we should have fancier foods in the general store, like that weird duck stuff you put on crackers."

"Foie gras," Lucky said.

"Blech!" Abigail stuck out her tongue. Then she leaned against Boomerang. "Pru and I couldn't figure out why the town council chose Maricela's speech. But Pru never accused Maricela of cheating or anything." Abigail lowered her voice to a whisper. "But I think maybe she cheated. Maybe her dad told the council they had to choose her speech *or else*." She widened her eyes.

"Or else?"

"Yeah. You know, like…" Abigail cleared her throat, then mimicked the mayor's loud voice. "If you don't choose my daughter's speech, I will force every member of this council to attend *all* of Maricela's piano recitals, and *all* of her singing recitals." She giggled.

That would be a terrible fate, but would the mayor do such a thing?

"There was also the time when Pru and Maricela tried out for the school play. Pru practiced her audition for weeks and she was really good. She has a pretty singing voice. Anyway, I went with Pru to the audition and somehow, when the piano started playing, Pru got off-key. Way off-key. Maricela ended up with the lead."

"Do you think she got off-key because she was nervous?" Lucky asked.

"Maybe." Abigail looked around, then leaned close to Lucky and spoke in a conspiratorial tone. "But maybe something else happened. The piano player is Maricela's private teacher, so it's possible she sabotaged the audition." She shrugged. "But we have no proof, and I'm not one to spread rumors."

Lucky was beginning to understand. Pru was a competitive person who always strove to do her best. She wasn't a poor sport when it came to losing, as long as the losing was fair and square. But if Pru believed that Maricela had an unfair advantage, or had cheated in some way, then no wonder Pru was so frustrated.

This was a tricky situation. Of course Lucky wanted to support Pru and her feelings. But she also wanted to make things better at school and do a great job on this project. How could she fix this?

On Monday, she was supposed to walk to school with Maricela. That would give them time alone. Maricela seemed to want to be Lucky's friend. Could Lucky convince her to change her mind about the group project?

Spirit nudged her from her thoughts. "Yes," she told him. "Let's go for a ride!"

13

Spirit's eyes flew open. He turned his ears front, then back, trying to pinpoint the direction of the noise that had awoken him.

Earlier, he and his girl had taken a nice ride, and when they'd returned, he'd headed into the barn for a drink of water. He wandered into his stall, intending to take a brief nap. He'd wake long before twilight so he could get back to the herd.

But Spirit hadn't realized that he was more tired than usual. It took more energy to ride in the cold air, and thus he'd slept longer than he'd intended.

What was that sound?

Chica Linda paced in the stall next to him, her ears flicking back and forth. Boomerang neighed in a high-pitched way. Somewhere, chickens were squawking. Something had agitated them.

Spirit pushed open his door and stepped outside.

Twilight had descended. The first stars were out, twinkling in the clear sky. The ground sparkled here and there with ice crystals. The chickens squawked again.

Spirit flared his nostrils. He knew that scent.
Wolves!

He turned and ran toward the sounds, which had erupted into chaos. Squawking, screeching, cries of terror as the chickens tried to save their lives. He ran across the street, around a house, and into the backyard, where he skidded to a stop. Three pairs of yellow eyes turned and looked at him. The wolves had been circling the chicken coop, trying to dig beneath the fence. It was rare to see wolves this close to town. Wolves detested people and preferred the dense coverage of the forest. Only one thing would bring them here.

Hunger.

Spirit understood the wolves' need for food, but his instinct was to protect. He reared on his hind legs, then brought his front legs down with a thud, purposely missing the nearest wolf by mere inches. A warning. The creature crouched. It pulled back its lips, fangs bared. Spirit reared again, landing even closer to the wolf and releasing a bugling neigh.

The wolves turned and ran.

From the corner of his eye, Spirit caught the glow of lanterns, followed by the sound of human voices.

He watched the wolves retreating, their gray bodies disappearing into the night. They were headed away from town. Back to the forest. Back toward the river.

Back toward Spirit's herd. Back toward the foals.

As the lanterns approached, Spirit broke into a gallop!

14

Maricela marched up the porch steps and knocked
on the Prescotts' front door. While waiting, she smoothed
her green coat, then shook a leaf off her black boot. She'd
brushed her hair one hundred times, as her mother had
taught her, and she'd tied it back with a white ribbon,
which contrasted nicely with her auburn waves. But then
her mother had insisted on a wool hat, which had ruined
the whole look. Stupid winter. How was anyone supposed
to look stylish in all these layers?

Muffled steps sounded inside. Maricela shuffled in
place, trying to stay warm. Her father had offered to take
her to school in the wagon, where she could snuggle
under a blanket, but she'd insisted on walking. She
wanted this time, alone, with Lucky.

The door opened. "Hello, Maricela." The smiling face
belonged to Cora Prescott. Maricela smiled back.

"Hello, Miss Prescott. I'm here to collect Lucky. We're
walking to school."

Cora seemed puzzled. Her eyes widened. "Really?
Together?"

"Yes. *Together*." Maricela didn't appreciate Cora's

reaction. Why was this so surprising? As if they shouldn't be friends, or as if it would be weird for them to be friends. Maricela and Lucky were from similar backgrounds, with similar upbringings. There was no one else in this backwoods town who was better suited to be Maricela's friend. She just needed more time to persuade Lucky to accept this fact.

"Come in," Cora said, waving Maricela inside. The house smelled like pancakes. A pot of coffee percolated on the potbelly stove. Cora walked to the bottom of the stairs and called, "Lucky!" Then she smiled again at Maricela. "I'm sure she'll be down in a moment."

"I certainly hope she doesn't take too long," Maricela said. "I'm supposed to deliver Lucky to school on time. Did you know that she has the worst attendance record in school, on account of her tardiness?"

Cora pressed her fingertips together and looked directly into Maricela's blue eyes. "While I appreciate honesty, Maricela, tattle-telling is not an admirable pastime for a young lady." Then she began to clear breakfast dishes from the kitchen table.

Maricela glowered for a moment. Tattle-telling was something little kids did. She'd simply been providing information. Surely an aunt would want to know about her niece's behavior so she could offer proper instruction. Maricela was about to argue this point when a loud stomping sound drew her attention. Lucky scrambled down the stairs. "I'm almost ready," she announced as she shoved her arms into her coat. Her long brown hair clearly hadn't been brushed one hundred times—maybe not even one time. Lucky darted past Maricela and grabbed her lunch bag off the counter. She planted a quick kiss on her aunt's cheek. "Bye," she said. Then she grabbed a pancake. "Want one?" she asked.

"No, thank you," Maricela said. Though the pancake looked delicious, she wasn't going to eat it with her fingers. Besides, she was wearing brand-new gloves.

"Suit yourself," Lucky said with a shrug, then folded the pancake in half and ate it in two big bites.

"Hold on," Cora said when Lucky was done chewing. "You're not leaving with only a coat!" She wrapped a scarf around Lucky's neck. "And this." She set a hat on her head. "Oh, maybe another scarf?"

"Aunt Cora, I won't be able to see or breathe if you keep putting layers on me."

Cora laughed. "You're right. I'm getting carried away." She hugged her niece.

Lucky opened the door. Then she glanced over her shoulder at Maricela. "Come on or we'll be late."

"We will *not* be late. I've timed it perfectly," Maricela said as she followed her outside.

"Have a nice day, you two," Cora called before shutting the door.

A chilling breeze blew across their exposed faces as they walked down the Prescott driveway. Maricela was glad she'd worn a pair of long underwear under her long skirt. Lucky, on the other hand, wore pants, as usual. "Why don't you wear dresses?" Maricela asked.

"I do. Sometimes. Well, on special occasions." Lucky pushed the scarf from her mouth. "Why don't you wear pants?"

"You, of all people, should know the answer to that question," Maricela said.

"Yeah, I know," Lucky mumbled. "Not *ladylike*."

"Exactement," Maricela said. "That's French for 'exactly so.'"

When they'd first met, Lucky had looked like the sophisticated city girl she was supposed to be—a girl who'd come from an influential and respected family, and attended a prestigious finishing school. But it hadn't taken long for Lucky to start looking like everyone else in Miradero. So disappointing.

But the most disappointing thing of all was that it hadn't taken Lucky long to become horse crazy, just like the rest of them. And Maricela placed the blame entirely on Pru Granger!

Pru. Maricela scowled just thinking about her. Everyone liked Pru. She had lots of friends. When Maricela was the new girl in town, she'd tried really hard to be friends with Pru. But Pru was always too busy with her ranch duties or with her horse activities. Then Maricela had tried really hard to be friends with Abigail, who liked looking through fashion catalogs and listening to the latest records on the Victrola. It looked as if that friendship might bloom. But Pru kept getting in the way with all that horse stuff! It started to feel as if Pru was taking Abigail away on purpose. So Maricela made a plan. She'd do everything she could to prove that she was better than Pru. Even if it meant getting her father to throw his weight around. Even if it meant cheating.

Served Pru right for taking Abigail away, and for not being her friend. *I deserve friends!*

"Why don't you like horses?" Lucky asked.

"Huh?" Lucky's question pulled Maricela from her thoughts of revenge.

"I'm just wondering why you don't like horses." Lucky stopped walking. "Did something happen? Are you afraid of them?"

"I'm *not* afraid," Maricela insisted. She wasn't about to admit the real reason she didn't like them. "I simply have no interest. They're smelly, dumb animals. That's all. Now hurry up. I have to keep my perfect attendance record."

They walked past the blacksmith's shop, the air clanging with the sound of metal against metal. Lucky looked at Maricela and opened her mouth to speak, but Maricela raised her hand to stop her. "You're not going to talk me into doing Pru's project, so don't even try. I'm not one bit interested in studying horses."

"But we'd study other animals, too. You've got to admit it's an interesting idea. Where do animals find food when everything is covered in snow? How do they drink if the water is frozen? How do they stay warm? Don't you wonder about those things?"

Maricela did love animals. For a moment, the project sounded interesting. But then Maricela pictured Pru's face, smug with the satisfaction of getting her way. "Not interested."

"We're supposed to tell Miss Flores what we're studying. She said she wanted to know on Monday. Today. So we need to make a decision."

"I already made my decision," Maricela said. "You three need to realize that winter fashion is an excellent topic."

They walked in silence the rest of the way. Lucky was frowning. Not a good sign. Maricela didn't want to alienate Lucky. There had to be another angle she could try, one that wouldn't involve doing what Pru wanted. When they reached the school steps, Maricela scooted in front of Lucky and smiled nicely at her. "Lucky, if you can persuade Pru to do the winter fashion project, then we'll have so much fun. We can go through all of my mom's fashion catalogs, and you can even try on all her fur coats." She waited for Bianca and Mary Pat to get up the stairs. They were wrapped in so many layers they waddled like ducks. Alone again, Maricela smiled as sweetly as she could. "You may have noticed that I'm Miss Flores's favorite student. If I tell her that you got us all to agree to the winter fashion project, she'd be impressed by your leadership skills. You might even get extra points."

Maricela waited, certain that Lucky would see the

logic in this choice. But Lucky kept frowning. "I'll try to get us all to agree…on something."

When they walked into the classroom, Miss Flores looked up from her desk and smiled with surprise. "I told you I'd bring her on time," Maricela boasted.

"Yes, you did. Good job, you two."

Maricela leaned close to Lucky and whispered, "You see, stick with me and you'll get into her good graces."

Perhaps there was still a chance they could be best friends.

15

"We were outside last night, mapping the night sky, when the chickens started squawking," Turo explained. "I grabbed a lantern and ran to see what was going on." Lucky, Pru, and Abigail stood next to Turo as he showed them the damage to his chicken coop. "They almost got under the fence. If they'd dug any deeper, we would have lost the entire flock."

Lucky looked at the hole. "*What* almost got under the fence?"

"Was it a badger?" Abigail asked. "Badgers can be real mean."

Lucky had never seen a badger, but she knew they had bandit-like faces and nasty teeth.

"It was a wolf," Pru said as she walked around the pen. "Three wolves, to be precise." She knelt and pointed to the ground. Lucky peered over her shoulder at some large paw prints in the dirt.

"Wolves," both Abigail and Turo whispered. An eerie feeling crept up Lucky's spine. They'd said the word *wolves* the same way one might say *ghosts*.

"And look over here." Pru led them to another set of prints. "See the way they go in this direction? A horse chased them off."

"A horse?" Abigail said. "But all the horses are in their barns at night. And besides, horses don't chase wolves. It's the other way 'round."

Pru smiled. "This particular horse doesn't live in a barn."

"Spirit?" Lucky asked. "How do you know it was Spirit?"

"Look at the hoofprints. This horse doesn't wear shoes."

Lucky smiled proudly. Of course Spirit was the one to chase the wolves away! But then her brows knotted. "Oh no, do you think he got hurt?" Once again, he hadn't been waiting for her after school. "Turo, did you see him?"

Turo shook his head. "No, I didn't see anything. Just my chickens running around in a panic." He pushed his thick brown hair from his face. "Spirit saved my flock!"

Lucky gazed into the distance hoping to see a buckskin stallion, his black mane flying as he galloped toward her. *Spirit, where are you?* A hand gently settled on her arm. She turned to find Abigail's big blue eyes looking at her. This time she didn't say *don't worry* or *it will be okay*. Because this time there was a real possibility that Spirit was hurt.

"Spirit is a huge stallion. Those wolves wouldn't stand a chance against him," Pru said. "But if he doesn't show up tomorrow, we'll help you look for him." Lucky nodded. She could always count on her friends to understand and to help.

Turo scratched the back of his neck as he examined one of the holes. "I've got to fix this damage right away or other critters might get in. Seems like everyone wants to eat chicken."

"Yum. I love fried chicken," Abigail said.

As if not appreciating this comment, the chickens squawked loudly. Even though the wolf attack had taken place hours before, they still appeared ruffled as they huddled together in their nesting boxes. There were eight total—four yellow, four red. "Oh, poor babies," Abigail said. "They're still scared."

"I'll need to take down this entire fence," Turo said, "and bury the new fencing deeper into the ground in case the wolves come back."

"Why don't we put the chickens into our barn, just to keep them safe while you're working?" Pru offered.

"Sure, that sounds good to me."

Turo found three wooden crates. They scooped the hens out of the nesting boxes and set two inside each crate. While Lucky, Pru, and Abigail carried the crates to the Grangers' barn, Turo remained behind to repair his fence.

Al Granger was riding past, on his way into town. "Hello, Pru. Howdy, Lucky and Abigail. Whatcha got there?"

"Turo's coop was attacked by wolves last night," Pru told him. "We're going to watch his hens for a while."

"That's mighty nice of you." Al pulled the reins, halting his horse. Then he looked down at the girls. "I just heard that Widow Brown's rabbit pen was also attacked. The wolves didn't get in but they caused a lot of damage."

"I've never seen a wolf," Lucky said, her arms wrapped around one of the crates. The hens inside clucked quietly.

"We don't often see them around here," Al said.

"Unlike coyotes, wolves tend to stay away from people. I reckon this cold weather is making food scarce. They must be mighty hungry to come into town."

"Are they dangerous?" Lucky asked. "I mean, could they attack a person?"

"I've never known them to, but if an animal gets hungry, there's no telling what it might do. Hunger is a powerful force."

"Dad, Spirit chased the wolves away," Pru said.

"Did he, now?" Al Granger rubbed his mustache. "Well, that doesn't surprise me. He's quite the horse."

"Do wolves attack horses?" Lucky asked. "I mean, could the wild herd be in danger?"

"Young foals, yes. If the wolves are in a pack, then any foal or injured horse could become prey."

"Injured?" Lucky gasped. She turned to Pru and Abigail. "We've got to go look for him."

Al frowned. "You think Spirit is injured? Was there any blood at the scene?"

"No blood," Pru said.

"Then I wouldn't be worried if I were you. I'm guessing Spirit's not here because he's sticking with his herd, keeping them safe. No wolf is gonna attack a healthy mustang. And I know firsthand that Spirit has one powerful kick!"

Al's words made Lucky feel better. He would know, better than she, what a wolf was capable of. Most likely, Spirit wasn't in Miradero because he was sticking with his herd. Lucky had seen the foals from afar. Spirit was protecting them.

Al coaxed his horse a bit closer to the girls. "Now listen up, you three. Don't you go getting the notion to go looking for Spirit, especially after twilight. He can take care of himself. I don't want you out there in the dark if we've got a wolf pack looking for food. You hear what I'm saying?" The PALs nodded. "Good." He adjusted his riding gloves, then gave his horse a gentle kick and rode off.

"I don't know why he's so worried," Pru grumbled. "We can take care of ourselves."

Lucky wasn't so sure. How do you protect yourself against a hungry wolf? Or wolves?

They carried the crates into the barn and released the hens into an empty stall. Abigail grabbed some straw and made nests for them. Pru scattered cracked corn while Lucky filled a bowl with water. The hens immediately began pecking at the corn, strutting and making happy little noises. Chica Linda and Boomerang stuck their heads over the stall wall and snorted, but the chickens were more interested in the corn than in the huge, furry faces staring down at them.

"I wonder what their names are," Abigail asked. Then she proceeded to give them all temporary names, based on their color. "Yellowy, Buttery, Corncob, Sunshine, Reddy, Cherry, Apple, and Strawberry." She scooped Strawberry into her arms. "This one's my favorite."

It occurred to Lucky that since they were offering the hens a safe place to stay, they might as well help Widow Brown with her rabbits. "Good idea," Pru said. So they headed out.

The widow lived in the middle of town, close to the office of JP & Sons Railroad. As the PALs walked, they discussed their school project. "It was really nice of Miss Flores to extend our deadline," Abigail said.

"But this is our last chance," Lucky said. "If we can't get Maricela to agree to something by Friday, we're all going to fail."

Lucky's father was sitting in his office when the girls walked past. They waved at him. He opened his office window. "What are you three up to? How come you're not riding?"

"Spirit isn't here," Lucky explained, and then she told her dad the story.

"Wolves?" He scowled. "I don't like the sound of that. I don't want you girls walking around after dark. I'm sure your parents would agree."

"We'll be careful," Pru assured him. "But right now we're going to Widow Brown's house to get her bunnies. Her rabbit pen was also attacked."

"I'll help. I need to stretch my legs, but I can't be gone too long. So much work to do." Jim closed the window, then grabbed his coat, scarf, and gloves and walked the short distance to Widow Brown's. Lucky hadn't yet met the widow, and she'd expected an elderly woman dressed in black, given her title, but Margaret Brown was a lovely woman about Cora's age. Despite the cold, she wore a pretty floral dress with a knitted cardigan. "Why, hello there, Mr. Prescott," she said with a wide grin. Why was she blinking so much? And why did she keep smoothing out her hair? "To what do I owe this pleasure?"

"Hello, Margaret," Jim said, smiling back. He removed his hat. "I'm just here to help my daughter, Lucky, and her friends. They heard you had a run-in with some wolves."

"Yes, we came to help you with your rabbits," Lucky said.

"Well, that's very kind of you to take care of my bunnies," Margaret said. "Those wolves made a real mess of their fence, so I've been keeping them in my kitchen."

They followed her into the tiny kitchen, where three black-and-white bunnies sat huddled in the corner. The girls each picked one up. Lucky's was a real fighter and it tried to get free, so she had to wrap her arms real tightly, but gently, and hold it close to her chest.

"Jim, would you like a cup of tea?" Margaret asked.

"That sounds nice," Jim said.

"Dad, don't you have to get back to work?" Lucky asked. "Didn't you say you just needed to stretch your legs but that you couldn't be gone too long?"

"I certainly said that." Jim put his hat back on his head. "Maybe some other time I can take you up on your offer of tea."

"Anytime, *Jim*," Widow Brown said, accentuating his name in a singsong way. Jim's cheeks turned red. Lucky frowned. "I make a succulent pot of chicken stew."

"Let's go," Lucky said, pushing her dad toward the door.

When they got to Jim's office, he gave Lucky a quick hug. "See you at supper. And remember, no walking around after dark."

They headed back to Pru's barn, holding the rabbits tightly. "Did you see that?" Lucky asked. "Did you see how Widow Brown was acting like she's in love with my dad?"

Abigail giggled. "Well, your dad *is* an eligible bachelor. At least that's what my mom calls him."

"Eligible bachelor?" Lucky snorted. "No he isn't." Pru and Abigail exchanged a look, which Lucky caught. "He isn't!"

"But he's not married," Pru said. "So that makes him a bachelor."

Lucky needed to set them straight, right here, right now. "A bachelor is someone who hasn't been married, and my dad already was married. And he doesn't want to get married again, so that means he's not eligible. Your mom is wrong. Plain and simple."

"Okay, okay," Pru said. "Don't get your reins in a tangle. Yeesh."

"Sorry, Lucky, I didn't mean to upset you," Abigail said.

Lucky sighed. "You didn't upset me. But that Widow Brown just better realize that she's barking up the wrong tree. My dad is not *eligible*."

Back at the barn, they set the rabbits in the same stall with the chickens. They added more straw and a few carrots. "We forgot to ask their names," Abigail said. Then she proceeded to name them. "You'll be Black-and-Whitey, you'll be Licorice, and you'll be Zebra."

"I wonder how many more creatures the wolves will try to eat," Pru said.

With that question, Lucky forgot all about Widow Brown and, once again, turned her thoughts to Spirit. *Please be okay.* She leaned against the barn wall and stared at the door. *Please be okay.* "Pru, what if…?"

"I'm way ahead of you," Pru said. She brushed straw off her pants, then grabbed her saddle. "You can ride with me." She didn't need to explain. Lucky knew exactly what Pru was offering. They'd go look for Spirit! Lucky began to slide the bridle over Chica Linda's head. Chica Linda stomped her back hoof, as if eager to help.

"But we're not supposed to go out after dark," Abigail reminded them.

"We've got at least one hour until dusk." Pru handed Abigail her saddle. "You in?"

"Of course we're in! Boomerang loves Spirit, too!"

Lucky wanted to hug them both, but there was no time to waste. As she slid open the barn door, dusk was waiting behind the mountains, ready to pounce like a hungry wolf.

16

Althea tied her sash across her shoulder. *Miradero Ladies' Aid Society President.* She'd carried the title for five years, ever since she'd founded the organization. Sash in place, she quickly assessed the lobby. A fire crackled in the stone hearth, nicely warming the space. The table was laden with sugar cookies, raisin scones, and china teacups ready to be filled with Tanglefoot Inn's signature plum tea. She glanced outside. Soon the membership would arrive for their Tuesday-night meeting. She ate a scone. Leadership required sustenance, as did public speaking. She ate another. There would be much to discuss.

The Tanglefoot Inn was the only inn in Miradero. It provided fancy rooms for out-of-town guests, practical rooms for traveling salesmen, and affordable rooms with bunk beds for temporary railroad workers. Gold-framed mirrors lined the walls. A massive portrait of Althea hung above the reception desk, greeting all who entered. Althea was extremely proud of her inn. She was born to be a businesswoman. Maybe she'd run for government one day, perhaps as town mayor. She could certainly do a better job than Mayor Gutierrez, who seemed more concerned with shaking hands and getting votes than with fixing roads and attracting new residents to Miradero. But for now she was busy running the inn and overseeing the society.

"Howdy," she greeted as the women began to stream through the door. The bellhop gathered their jackets, hats, and scarves and hung them on the rack. They helped themselves to cups of tea, cookies, and scones. Almost every woman in town belonged to the society, and it was heartwarming to see that they'd begun to include their daughters. Althea fully believed that it was never too early to learn about community service.

Miss Flores took a seat, as did Widow Brown. "Be sure to help yourselves to some sweets," Althea said to Mrs. Gutierrez and her daughter, Maricela. They each took a cookie, but Mrs. Gutierrez made a comment about the lack of Danish pastries in Miradero. Althea laughed to herself. *Such highfalutin ways*, she thought. Those two wore their snobbery like pigs wore mud. They weren't Althea's favorite people, but in the end, the Gutierrez family did help raise money for various causes and they did come through when needed. So Althea ignored the rude comment about her cookies, which had been made by her kitchen staff.

Fanny Granger and her daughter, Pru, walked in, along with Abigail and her mother, followed by Cora Prescott and her niece, Lucky. Lucky, Pru, and Abigail immediately formed a tight circle. "Have you seen him?" Pru asked. Lucky shook her head, her expression tense with worry.

Althea stepped close to Cora. "What's wrong with Lucky?"

"Her wild horse hasn't been seen in two days."

Althea nodded. "Lovin' something wild usually brings heartache." She was referring to a few wandering cowboys she'd met over the years. "Some creatures just can't be tamed."

Soon the lobby was filled with women who were engaged in conversation and sipping tea. Althea glanced at the clock, then clapped her hands. "All right, ladies, let's not dillydally. It's time to get started." The women settled onto divans, chairs, and stools, with the younger girls sitting on the plush carpet. Then they all quieted and waited for Althea to speak again.

"Welcome, everyone." She went through the formalities of bringing the meeting to order, with Cora seconding the motion. Then the society's secretary, Miss Flores, took roll. "As we discussed at our last meeting, we're all concerned about this cold spell we've been having. If things get worse, and I reckon they will, we could be facing some mighty difficult circumstances." Audience members nodded. While everyone seemed attentive, Lucky kept staring out the window. *Poor thing,* Althea thought. *She's far too young to be fretting so.*

Althea continued. "We voted that we'd help those members of our community who might not have the means, or who might be too old to take care of themselves." More nodding. "So let's make a list of those people."

"Our neighbor, Mr. Washington, can barely walk," Mrs. Perkins pointed out. "On account of his rheumatism."

"And my mother-in-law can't see more than two feet in front of her, but she insists on living in that old house of hers, alone," said Mrs. Thayer.

A few more names were mentioned. Althea smiled, so proud to be a part of this caring community. "As we agreed, our next mission, ladies, is to make care packages for our vulnerable citizens and deliver them this week." As treasurer, Cora confirmed that there were available funds thanks to their sales of corn on the cob at the harvest festival.

Discussion ensued, lists were made, duties were assigned, and an hour later, feeling the satisfaction of a job well done, Althea called the meeting to a close.

The membership bundled themselves up and headed back outside. After most everyone had left, Lucky, Pru, and Abigail were once again gathered in a huddle. "What are you girls discussing?" Althea asked.

"We were thinking, while you're making care packages for the people of Miradero, maybe we could make care packages for the animals," Abigail said.

Fanny Granger looked up from buttoning her coat. "Abigail, that's an excellent idea."

Abigail put her arm around Pru's shoulder. "Actually, we all came up with it."

"Miss Flores wants us to do a group project with a winter theme," Lucky said. "Pru thought it would be interesting to study how animals survive in winter."

"But Maricela's in our group and she won't do that," Pru explained.

"But we could do a Ladies' Aid Society project without Maricela," Abigail said.

Althea nodded. "Care packages for the critters. I

really like this idea. It's so clever, it might win you a ribbon from our society's national chapter."

"You could make suet cones for the birds. They can have a lot of trouble finding food in the winter," Fanny told them. "And you could make seed cakes for the smaller animals, like rabbits and mice."

"I was also thinking about the mustang herd," Lucky said. "Can we do something for them?"

Fanny thought about it for a moment. "It's possible, but they tend to travel a lot during the winter months. They might not even be around."

"Travel?" Lucky took a deep breath. "Do you think that's what happened? That the herd traveled far away? Is that why I haven't seen Spirit?"

"They will go as far as they need to find food," Fanny said, handing Pru her coat.

Lucky sighed. Althea could tell she was trying to put on a brave face. If Althea had a daughter, she'd want her to be just like Lucky—strong body, strong mind, strong spirit. A girl after her own heart.

"Let's start making the care packages right away!" Lucky said.

Althea slapped her thigh. "By gum, I couldn't be prouder of you girls, thinkin' about the critters. We don't want anyone to go hungry this winter. We're all vulnerable when nature turns harsh."

Once everyone had gone, Althea called her waitstaff over and they began to collect the dirty plates and teacups. But movement caught the corner of Althea's eye. She glanced across the lobby. Maricela grabbed her coat and scurried outside. Apparently, she'd been standing behind the coat tree, unnoticed. Althea narrowed her eyes. Clearly, Maricela had been hiding. And eavesdropping.

What was she up to?

17

As Lucky's eyes fluttered open, she stretched her legs until her toes reached the end of the bed. Then she yawned and lazily rolled over. Why was it so quiet? And what was that odd brightness peeking between the curtains?

Wait. Could it be?

She scrambled out of bed and ran to the window. As she pulled the curtains open, she gasped with wonder. Snow! From her front yard to the distant mountains, all of Miradero was covered in a sparkling winter blanket. But the best thing of all was the trail of hoofprints leading up the driveway all the way to the front porch. Lucky couldn't see beneath the peaked roof, but she knew who was waiting below.

This wasn't the city, with its slippery sidewalks and frozen puddles. There was no way Cora would make Lucky stay inside, would she? Lucky wasn't about to find out. She raced downstairs and threw open the door. "Spirit!"

There he stood, at the bottom of the porch steps,

shaggier than ever. He dipped his head in greeting and smiled at her with his eyes. Lucky didn't care how cold it was. She stumbled down the steps and wrapped her arms around his neck, only this time she held on longer than usual. "Where have you been?" she asked. He smelled different, not so much like grass and dirt, but more like fresh, crisp air. Like winter. She walked around him, searching for signs that he'd been hurt by those wolves. To her relief, he seemed perfectly fine.

"Fortuna Esperanza Navarro Prescott, you get in here before you catch your death of cold!" Cora ordered from the doorway.

"Stay there," Lucky told Spirit. "I'll be right back."

Cora tightened the belt on her bathrobe. "Whatever is the matter with you, going outside in your nightgown and slippers? You were not raised in a barn, young lady."

Now that Lucky had spent countless hours in barns, she found this comment funny. Barns were perfectly lovely places. But she didn't argue this point as she raced back into the house. Cora turned her attention to the buckskin stallion. "Hello, Spirit," she said, as if he were in trouble, too. Spirit took a step forward, placing his hoof on the first step. "Oh no you don't," Cora said, wagging a finger at him. "I don't care how much she loves you; horses do *not* belong inside." She hurriedly shut the door.

"I've never seen anyone get dressed that fast," Jim said with a chuckle when, a few minutes later, Lucky flew back down the stairs and into the kitchen. He sat at the kitchen table, sipping his morning coffee.

"Do you think they'll open the schoolhouse this morning?" Cora asked. And right on cue, the town hall bell rang three times. Not the school bell, which had a higher, sweeter resonance. Three clangs from the deeper, more serious town hall bell meant that school was canceled. This had only happened twice since Lucky had moved to Miradero. The first time was because a few of the kids had caught frontier flu, which was very contagious, so the town council voted to close the school for a whole week. The second time was when Miss Flores got sick from a bad batch of chili.

"No school!" Lucky cried. The entire day stretched before her. With Spirit! She tied her boots, then reached for the doorknob.

"Coat!" Cora said.

"I know, I know." Lucky yanked her coat off the rack. She threw it on, then reached for the knob again.

"Hat!" Cora said, tapping her foot on the floor.

"Yeah, yeah." Lucky grabbed it.

"You might want a scarf," Jim added with bemusement.

Oh for goodness' sake. Why was everyone trying to slow her down? "Fine!" She found her scarf and wound it around her neck. "May I go *now*?" While Jim chuckled at his daughter's impatience, Cora was still tapping that foot with annoyance. She pointed to a bench.

"You can't seriously think I'm going to let you ride off in the snow without gloves?" she said.

Lucky whipped around, grabbed the gloves, then was outside before Cora could utter another word. "Hurry," she told Spirit as she grabbed his mane and jumped onto his back. "Before she makes me eat breakfast!" Who needed breakfast when there was snow and a wild mustang waiting?

Lucky had never ridden a horse in the snow. And as far as she knew, Spirit had never carried a person through the snow. It was a very different feeling for each of them. He had to lift his legs higher, resulting in an odd gait. And they moved slower than usual, which was fine with Lucky. She took in the beautiful sight. It was as if a blanket of quiet had fallen over the world. Even the birds weren't singing. She squinted against the brightness, but after a while her eyes adjusted. Other than Spirit's hoofprints, there were no other prints. Critters were staying in their burrows.

They rode to a hilltop and looked out over the serene wonderland. Just the two of them. Spirit's ears turned left, then right, catching the sounds of kids emerging from their houses, squealing with delight. All around them, the town came to life.

They headed to the barn, hoping to find Pru and Abigail.

Chica Linda and Boomerang were outside the barn, playfully prancing in the snow. Pru was shoveling snow from the barn's entrance, to make it easier to get in and out. Abigail was using a rake handle to break the ice in the horses' drinking trough.

"Hi, Spirit!" Pru called.

"Oh, Spirit, it's so good to see you," Abigail said, hugging him the way Lucky always did.

Lucky slid off Spirit's back. "You need help?" she asked.

"Sure, there's another shovel." Pru pointed to the side of the barn. Lucky grabbed the shovel and joined Pru.

"Can you believe this?" Abigail asked. "Mom says it's the most snow she's ever seen in Miradero."

Boomerang pranced past, kicking up snow. "They're acting like yearlings," Pru said with a laugh as he chased Chica Linda around a tree. His movement knocked a clump of snow off a branch. The clump landed on Spirit's head. Spirit shook off the snow, then, glaring through his shaggy forelock, began to chase Boomerang.

"So cute," Abigail said.

"Hey, let's all go for a ride," Lucky suggested.

"We have to wait for Turo," Pru explained. "He's going to put studded horseshoes on Chica Linda and Boomerang so they won't slip. See, look…" She lifted Chica Linda's front hoof. Lucky leaned close. "With a normal shoe, the snow gets packed up in there and it gets slippery. Spirit doesn't have to worry because he doesn't wear shoes."

"So no ride?" Lucky asked, disappointed.

"Not until later. Turo has a lot of horses waiting for him today."

Spirit, Chica Linda, and Boomerang continued their playful antics, jumping and prancing around. Sticking their noses into the snow, then sneezing.

Lucky and Pru had cleared a wide path, so they set the shovels aside. "I'm so glad they canceled school," Pru said.

"Maybe there won't be school tomorrow," Abigail said. "Or the next day. Maybe it will never stop snowing." She grabbed a handful of snow, pressed it into a ball, then began to roll the ball across the yard. Lucky and Pru joined her, each rolling a section of what would become a snowman.

"When we're done here, let's start making those care packages," Lucky said. "At my house." She lifted her snowball and stuck it on top of Abigail's.

"Sounds good. But that doesn't solve our other problem." Pru frowned, then set her smaller snowball on top. "We still don't have a group project."

Abigail grabbed two rocks and pushed them into the top snowball for eyes. "If only Maricela would listen to us. We're going to have so much fun making those care packages. And the animals are going to be so happy."

After the girls had added two stick arms, a pinecone

nose, and had wrapped Pru's scarf around the snowman's neck, Chica Linda and Boomerang ambled over and sniffed the weird creation. But Spirit stuck his nose into the snow again, then dug with his front hoof. Was he looking for something? "I think he's trying to get to the grass," Lucky realized. "Are you hungry, boy?"

"Here." Abigail reached into her pocket and pulled out an oatmeal cookie, which Spirit gobbled up.

"He needs more." Lucky ran into the barn and dumped some oats into a pail. "I'm sorry, boy. I didn't know you were so hungry. I should have realized," she said, offering the meal to Spirit.

While Spirit ate, Boomerang tried to stick his nose into the pail. "Aw, cut it out, Boomerang," Abigail said as she pushed him away. "You already ate. Yeesh. Give someone else a chance."

Lucky took a quick breath. "Hey, I have an idea. We can make the suet cones for the birds, and the seed cakes for the small mammals, but what if we make Abigail's oatmeal cookies for Spirit's herd? Horses are crazy about those cookies." Just when she finished sharing her idea, a snowball hit her in the rump. Snips howled with laughter.

A snowball fight with Snips and his posse ensued, followed by a flurry of snow angel making. Then the PALs decided to head up to Lucky's house to start working on the care packages. Abigail left her brother with some wise advice: "Don't eat the yellow snow." As the girls led Chica Linda and Boomerang into the corral, a pair of farmers walked up, each holding something wrapped in a blanket.

"Hello, Mr. Miller," Pru said. "Whatcha got there?"

"The snow caved in my shed roof, so now my pygmy goats have no place to sleep. I heard you were taking care of animals." The little goat poked her white face from the blanket and bleated softly.

"I remember these goats from the harvest festival," Lucky said as she lifted the edge of the second farmer's blanket.

"They're so cute!" Abigail kissed both goats on the forehead.

"I have three sheep that also need a place. Just temporary, until this weather passes and I can fix the roof."

Pru shrugged. "Sure, we'd be happy to take care of them. If they don't mind sleeping with chickens and rabbits, there's plenty of room in our barn." Pru led them inside. "The more the merrier, I guess."

By the time the three sheep arrived, Lucky, Pru, and Abigail had prepared two more stalls with clean straw and water. Lucky put her hands on her hips and looked around. "You know, we've made our own Tanglefoot Inn," she mused, "only this one's for animals." Though it was loud, with all the bleating, snorting, and squawking, the noise was harmonious, as if all the creatures were happy to be together. "What do you think, Spirit?" She leaned against his neck. But he wasn't listening to her. Instead, he was gazing out the window.

He wanted to leave again; she could feel it. How many days would he be gone this time? It was so cold out there, and tonight it would be even colder. "Spirit, won't you stay here, where it's warm?"

He turned and looked into her eyes. Then he bowed his head and pressed his forehead against hers. "I know," she said. "You have to take care of your herd. It's okay; I understand." She did, but understanding didn't take away her worry. She slid open the barn door and motioned him through. "Go ahead."

Once again, he left, galloping off toward the river.

"He cares about his family," Pru said, setting her hand on Lucky's shoulder.

"I know."

What Lucky didn't know was that the wolves would howl that night. And she wouldn't sleep a wink.

18

As Spirit raced through the snow, the strange scents of people gradually faded, as if the wind were washing him clean. His legs grew tired. Galloping through the heavy powder was difficult. He veered to the right, then followed the trail he'd made earlier. The air stung the inside of his nostrils as he took great, deep breaths. The sooner he reached his herd, the sooner he'd be there to protect them. Wolves hunted at night, walking as quietly across the ground as a cloud drifts across the sky. Night was dangerous when predators were hungry. He quickened his pace.

No doubt the herd was also hungry. There was no satisfaction in eating frozen plants and tree bark. If only he could lead them to his girl. She'd feed them oats and hay. But he couldn't do that. The town was full of men with ropes—men who would catch the largest mustangs and lock them up behind fences. Those men couldn't be trusted. Spirit had learned that the hard way.

He followed the herd's scent. The horses were pressed up against a steep canyon wall, which offered protection from the wind. They greeted him as they began to settle in for the night. The colt lay next to his mother, already fast asleep. Spirit wound his way until he found his sister and her filly. The filly lifted her head and looked up at him. Her eyes were glassy. He sniffed her. She smelled different. He looked into his sister's eyes. She nodded sadly.

The filly was sick. Very, very sick.

Part Three

19

More snow fell overnight, but thanks to the grit and
determination of the townspeople, walkways were
shoveled and roads were packed down so the kids could
attend school. Just as Lucky was finishing breakfast, a
knock sounded on the door. She opened it to find Mayor
Gutierrez. "Why, hello there, Lucky," he said, whisking
off his bowler hat. Then he shook her hand in his usual,
eager way. "We've come to escort you to school."

"You have?" Lucky asked, a bit confused at first. But
then she remembered Maricela's deal with Miss Flores.
"Oh, right." With a bit of effort, she managed to pull her
hand away. "Thanks."

"Couldn't get the wagon up the drive," the mayor
explained. "Too steep in this snow." He pointed to the
bottom of the driveway, where his wagon and horse
waited. Maricela sat in the back seat, her face peeking
out from beneath a pile of blankets.

"Good morning, Mayor," Jim said. More vigorous
handshaking ensued. "Would you like to come in for a
cup of coffee?"

Mayor Guiterrez beamed. "I would indeed, Jim,

I would indeed. But I've promised Maricela not to dillydally. She is determined to get Lucky to school on time, and you know my daughter can be quite…" He paused, his smile fading. "Quite *determined*."

"Dad!" Maricela hollered.

Lucky wondered if *determined* was the best word choice. *Bossy* was more like it. "Yes, dear!" he hollered back. Then he smiled at Jim again. "I hope you don't think it's rude that I don't accept your offer of coffee. I'm always delighted to visit with local voters and discuss the matters of the day. Remember, a vote for Gutierrez is a vote for progress."

"*DAAAAAAD!*"

Lucky suddenly felt sorry for the mayor. She only had to deal with Maricela on a part-time basis, but he had to live with her. Lucky collected her outerwear and lunch bag, gave a quick kiss to Cora and Jim, then followed the mayor to his wagon. She climbed onto the bench seat.

"Good morning," Maricela said, lifting one of the blankets to make room for Lucky. It was nice and warm under there.

"Thanks for picking me up," Lucky said as Mayor Gutierrez climbed up front and took the reins.

144

"I'm always here for the people of Miradero." Why did he always sound like he was campaigning? Lucky wasn't even old enough to vote.

Maricela seemed in good spirits. As they cuddled together, Lucky realized that this was the perfect time to try, once again, to persuade Maricela to change her mind. "Maricela, about our school project…"

Maricela glared at Lucky, her mood instantly turning dark. "I don't want to talk about it."

"But we were supposed to know by Friday and that's tomorrow. If we don't figure something out, we're all going to fail."

"It's too cold to talk." She pulled the blanket all the way over her head. What was going on? Didn't Maricela, the teacher's pet, care about her grades?

"As the group leader, I—"

"We can talk about this later," Maricela said, her voice muffled by the blankets.

Later? Lucky didn't like being dismissed. Maricela was acting like she had something more important to think about.

"You girls warm back there?" the mayor asked, glancing over his shoulder.

"Yes, thank you," Lucky said. Then she pushed

off the blankets and scooted away from Maricela. She wasn't going to cuddle with someone who was being so pigheaded, no matter how cold it was outside!

They arrived at school on time. There'd been no sign of Spirit, but that didn't surprise Lucky. After thanking Mr. Gutierrez again, she jumped out of the wagon without waiting for Maricela and ran up the steps. She needed to talk to Pru and Abigail right away. They had to come to a decision before Miss Flores failed them.

Turo was stoking the fire when Lucky charged into the classroom. Miss Flores looked up from her desk. "Nice to see you on time, Lucky." She walked over to the attendance board and drew another star next to Lucky's name. Then she said, very quietly, "You know, I ran into your father at the bakery the other day. We had a very nice conversation. How is he?"

How is he? Why was Miss Flores asking about Lucky's father? "He's fine, I guess," Lucky said with a shrug.

"Oh, that's nice." Miss Flores smiled sweetly. "I was wondering…." Why were her cheeks turning red? "Please tell him I said hello." She turned briskly on her heels and walked back to her desk.

"That was weird," Lucky whispered to Pru and Abigail as she took her seat.

"I told you," Abigail chirped. "Your dad is an eligib—"

"Don't say it," Lucky grumbled.

After everyone was seated, including Maricela, Miss Flores called upon Lucky. "Lucky, I'm hoping that you and your group will have a decision tomorrow regarding your winter project." She folded her hands and waited. Lucky slowly stood. As the leader, she felt like a complete failure.

"Well, Miss Flores, we're still having trouble agreeing. You see, it's still three against one. Maricela wants to—"

Maricela darted to her feet. "Lucky was about to say that Maricela wants to make winter care packages for animals. You know, like suet cones for the songbirds and little seed cakes for rabbits and mice. And I'm pretty sure that the rest of my team will agree because why wouldn't they want to help animals?" Lucky's mouth fell open. Wait a minute. How did Maricela know about their plan to feed the animals? They hadn't told her.

Miss Flores smiled. "I think that's a great idea, Maricela." Maricela puffed out her chest until it looked like she might pop a button.

"Wait a minute." Pru jumped to her feet, too. "That idea was Abigail's, not Maricela's."

Maricela released a high-pitched, nervous sort of laugh. "Don't be silly, Pru. You know how much I love animals. I love them all, so much. Why wouldn't I want to help them? And since I came up with the winning idea, I think I should be leader."

"Leader?" Pru said. "She'll make a terrible leader. She doesn't listen to anyone. She only wants to do things her way!"

Abigail raised her hand. "Miss Flores, I like having Lucky as our leader."

"Pru, please sit down," Miss Flores said sternly. "I am very tired of the way you and Maricela are always bickering. Are you all in agreement that you'd like to make winter care packages for the animals?" Lucky, Pru, Abigail, and Maricela nodded. "Then it appears that Maricela did help to bring about an agreement, so why don't Maricela and Lucky move forward as co-leaders?"

"That's fine by me," Maricela said.

Lucky sighed. Having to share a leadership role with Maricela was not going to be fun, but handing over total power to her would be worse. "Okay," she agreed.

Pru slumped into her seat. "This is so typical of

Maricela," Pru whispered. "It wasn't her idea. She stole it, just like she steals everything."

"I don't really care who gets credit," Abigail whispered back. "I just want to help the animals."

Lucky realized that Abigail was possibly the sweetest person she'd ever met. Why bother battling with Maricela? The end result was the important thing—to feed the creatures that needed their help. And not getting an F on the project would be nice, too. But still, the fact that Maricela was taking credit for Abigail's idea seemed so unfair.

"Miss Flores," Lucky said, raising her hand. "Maricela forgot to mention that along with making suet cones for the birds, and seed cakes for the rodents, we're also going to make horse cookies for the mustang herd."

Maricela gasped. "I didn't—"

"Oh, but it was your idea, remember? You said you love all animals and that you wouldn't want any of them to go hungry. Because you love them, so much. Isn't that right?" Lucky waited. She'd put Maricela into a corner. With everyone watching, she had no choice but to agree, or else her lie would be exposed.

"Uh-huh," Maricela mumbled, her chest deflating as she slumped into her chair.

Lucky and Pru shared a satisfied smile. Maricela had taken advantage of Abigail. And she'd made it look as if Lucky had failed as the group leader. As if Maricela had swooped in on her angelic wings to save them all. What a load of horse manure! Lucky clearly hadn't earned any points with Miss Flores today. But at least they were on the right path.

20

On Friday after school, Lucky stood at the stove, warming lamb fat in a big cast-iron pot. The recipe for suet cones called for equal parts lamb fat and bird seed. "We have sunflower seeds, millet seeds, and cracked corn," Abigail said as she set the ingredients on the kitchen table.

"And here's a bucket of pinecones," Pru announced. "I had to dig for them under the snow, so I'm going to set them in front of the fire to dry."

The plan was to mix the seed and suet, then smear the paste into the spaces of an upside-down pinecone. Then they'd tie twine around the cone and hang it from a tree. "The birds are going to love this," Abigail said.

"That stuff stinks," Maricela complained from her perch on one of the Prescotts' kitchen stools. She'd been sitting the entire time, not lifting a finger. "I don't want to get my dress dirty. It came all the way from Chicago," she'd explained.

"Why would you wear a nice dress anyway?" Pru

asked. "You knew we were going to be working. You should have worn work clothes."

"I don't own work clothes. Why would I? We have a housekeeper who does all the work." She tucked her knees under her skirt. "Why don't you have a housekeeper, Lucky? Didn't you have one in Philadelphia?"

"We don't need one," Lucky said. "My dad, my aunt, and I all share the chores."

"Your housekeeper isn't here, Maricela, so you'd best roll up your sleeves and help," Pru said. The lamb fat had gently melted, so Lucky removed the pot from the stove. Then she and Abigail began to add the seeds.

Maricela tossed her hair behind her shoulders. "I don't see why I should work. You should all be grateful. If I hadn't agreed to make these care packages, we all would have failed."

"Grateful?" Pru said. Both Lucky and Abigail held their breaths. The last thing they needed was a big blowout between those two. There was so much work to be done. Once they'd finished the suet cones, they were going to make the seed cakes and the horse treats, which for Lucky were the most important part of the entire project. She needed to distract Pru and Maricela.

"Hey, Maricela," she said. "Cutting twine won't get your hands dirty. And we'd all be very grateful for the help." If she had to feed false flattery to her, then so be it. The afternoon was getting away from them and there was so much to do.

Maricela raised an eyebrow. "You see, it's not so hard to be nice." She grabbed the twine and scissors. Pru rolled her eyes, but didn't say anything. She also knew they needed Maricela's help.

Lucky and Pru scooped the birdseed mixture and began to fill the pinecones. They were huge cones, from a ponderosa pine, with large gaps between the scales. Cora popped into the kitchen. "I'm going to help Althea deliver care packages," she said. "You girls should be fine on your own, but no using the oven while I'm gone."

While the seed cakes weren't cakes in the usual sense and didn't require baking, the cookies did need twelve minutes in the oven. "But what about the cookies?" Lucky asked.

"The baking will have to wait until I return." And without further discussion, Cora hurried out the front door.

"We can still get the ingredients ready," Pru said, noticing the disappointed look on Lucky's face.

"Oh, that's a good idea." Abigail took a large bowl off the shelf.

Maricela stopped cutting twine. Her brows knotted. "Cookies?"

"For horses," Pru said.

"The horses love my regular oatmeal cookies, but these will be special, with horse-approved ingredients," Abigail explained.

"Mrs. Granger helped alter the recipe," Lucky said. "So we're using only flour, molasses, oats, raisins, and apples."

Maricela set the scissors aside with a loud *thunk*. "I don't care what they're made of. I told you from the very beginning I wanted nothing to do with horses."

Oh no, here we go, Lucky thought. "But this isn't a horse project. This is an *animal* project."

"And you agreed to do it," Pru said.

"Yes, but you tricked me into agreeing."

"And you tricked everyone into thinking it was your idea, remember?" Pru set her serving spoon on the table with an even louder *thunk*. Then she walked around the table until she was standing right next to Maricela. "I've been thinking about it, Maricela. Yes, it's possible that you and Abigail had the exact same idea. But it's doubtful. I mean, you kept talking about winter fashion. You didn't seem one bit interested in studying animals. But you were at the Ladies' Aid Society meeting, and that's where Abigail came up with her idea. Were you spying on us?"

Pru's explanation made sense, and Lucky suspected it was true.

Maricela's face went red. Then she slid off the bench and she and Pru stood, face-to-face, glaring at each other. If Althea were there, she'd probably say, *They look as mad as two badgers in a bucket!*

"So, you think I *spied* on you? I suppose you think I ruined your speech, too."

Pru's mouth fell open. "As a matter of fact, I do think that, but I wouldn't publicly accuse you because I don't have proof. And I was raised to think the best of people, unless they prove otherwise—and you proved otherwise, Maricela, when you took credit for Abigail's idea!"

"Look, I don't care whose idea it was," Abigail said. "Will you please stop fighting?"

"I care," Pru said. "Don't you get it? This is what

Maricela does. She stops at nothing to get her way. She'll do anything to beat me. Why? I never did anything to you, Maricela!" And before Lucky could say anything, Pru grabbed her coat and stomped out through the kitchen door.

"Wait!" Lucky called.

"I don't know what she's talking about," Maricela said, tears in her eyes. Then she grabbed her coat and followed in Pru's footsteps. Lucky and Abigail raced to the doorway and watched as Pru and Maricela marched down the driveway, side by side. Then Pru turned left toward her house, and Maricela turned right.

Lucky and Abigail sighed. "How are we going to finish all this work by ourselves?" Lucky asked.

"We can try," Abigail said, her usual optimistic self.

But even though they worked hard and fast enough to finish the suet cones, Abigail and Lucky didn't get to bake the horse cookies. At five o'clock, Abigail's dad came to pick her up.

"We have so much work left to do," Abigail told him. "Can't you pick me up later?" Mr. Stone explained that there would be another freezing spell that night, so it would be too cold for him to pick her up later. She and Lucky could work on their project tomorrow.

After Lucky hugged Abigail good-bye, a tight feeling settled in Lucky's stomach. She was mad at Maricela for quitting, but she was also mad at Pru. They were supposed to be a team. And now Spirit and his herd would go another day without their care packages.

21

Jim and Cora returned late that evening. Cora's deliveries had taken longer than expected and Jim had been finishing up some business at the JP & Sons' office. The suet cones were lined up on the porch so that the cold air could harden the suet. "What a lot of work you've accomplished," Cora said proudly. She and Jim wiped snow from their boots, then set them near the fireplace to dry.

"We have thirty cones for the birds and two dozen seed cakes for the rabbits and mice."

"If I didn't know better, I'd think a twister touched down in here," Jim said as he walked into the kitchen, where Lucky was still working. Now that she could use the oven, she was patting the mixture into mounds.

"I know we made a mess," she said. "I'll clean it up. I promise."

Lucky expected a sigh of exasperation from her aunt. Cora often said that tidiness was a virtue. But at that moment she ignored the mess. "I'm too tired to fret about it," she said, sinking onto the sofa. Then she yawned, without even covering her mouth. She *was* tired!

Jim sliced a loaf of bread, and heated up some split pea soup, a leftover from the previous evening's dinner. "It's nice to see you working so hard on schoolwork," he said, pulling Lucky away from her project. "But you need to eat." Reluctantly, Lucky washed her hands, then sat at the table. As Jim stirred his soup, steam rose above his bowl. "It seems Miss Flores has really gotten you into the swing of things at your new school."

"Miss Flores is a lovely woman," Cora said as she joined them. "When we first moved here, and I learned that there was only one teacher for the entire town, I was admittedly worried. But I've had a number of conversations with her about literature and social issues. She's very knowledgeable." Cora buttered a bread slice, then looked at Jim. "Did you know she's not married?"

Jim chuckled. "Why does everyone keep telling me who is and who isn't married? Am I wearing a sign on my back that says 'Looking for a Wife'?"

"Don't be silly, Jim. I only mention it because you are an eligible bachelor."

There was that term again. Lucky stirred her soup 'round and 'round, waiting for her father's reaction. Surely he'd laugh and say, *That's ridiculous! I'm not eligible, because I'm very happy being single and I don't need a wife.*

But he didn't say that. Instead he said, "Speaking of Miss Flores, I did run into her at the bakery. She does seem to be a very nice person." He smiled in a strange way, as if he'd just discovered a new flavor of ice cream.

"Did you speak to each other?" Cora asked.

"Yes; it was a short conversation, but I found her quite delightful."

Delightful? Lucky scowled. What was going on?

Jim sat back in his chair. "You know, I've been so busy at work, I haven't volunteered in your classroom yet. Perhaps I should stop by and—"

"No!" Lucky blurted, a chunk of carrot flying from her mouth.

"Esperanza!" her aunt chided. "Do not spit food across the table."

"Sorry." Lucky wiped her mouth with a napkin. "Dad, we don't need volunteers right now. We have too many volunteers. Really." That was a huge lie. Miss Flores had complained only a few days ago that she could use help clearing some fallen branches away from the schoolhouse. "Too many volunteers," Lucky repeated.

Jim helped himself to a slice of bread. "Yes, well, maybe some other time, when we don't have blizzards and avalanches threatening to close the railroad."

"Yeah, some other time." If Lucky had a choice, that other time would be *never*. Imagine if her dad started dating her teacher. How awkward would that be? She had enough troubles at school without adding *that* to the mix. And besides, he didn't need to date anyone. They were perfectly happy, the three of them. Nothing needed to change.

After dinner, Lucky went back to work on the cookies, but Cora stopped her. "That's enough for tonight, young lady."

"But, Aunt Cora—"

"Lucky, I admire your dedication to your schoolwork. But it is almost midnight. Besides, it wouldn't be safe to have you cooking on a wood stove all night long without supervision. I need to get some sleep."

"So do I," Jim said. He kissed Lucky's forehead. "Good night, sweet pea."

Even though she tried, three more times, to argue her case, her aunt and father refused to be swayed and insisted that everyone go to bed. Reluctantly, Lucky got into her pajamas. She wound her nightstand clock and set the alarm for five AM. It would still be dark, but she could sneak downstairs and start work again, maybe getting a couple batches of cookies baked. And then she and Pru and Abigail would hang the suet cones and scatter the seed cakes. Hopefully, some birds and rabbits, field mice, squirrels and chipmunks would have full bellies. Then the PALs could ride out to scatter the cookies for the herd.

As Lucky climbed into bed, Cora came into her room. "Lucky, are you going to tell me what's wrong?"

"I thought you wanted to go to sleep," Lucky said grumpily.

Cora adjusted her bathrobe, then sat on the bed. "You were a bit snappy at supper. That's not like you. What happened?"

Lucky told Cora about the fight between Pru and Maricela and how they'd both stormed out. "I know Maricela can be mean, but we needed her help. And Pru's help."

Cora nodded thoughtfully, then said, "Sometimes when people act mean, they are hurting inside. Maybe something is bothering Maricela."

"I can't imagine what could be bothering her. She gets her way all the time. And she has everything."

"Does she have everything?" Cora asked. Lucky wasn't sure how to answer that question. Maricela lived in a grand house, wore fancy clothes, brought gourmet lunches to school, and always had pocket money for candy at the general store.

"I'm mad at Pru, too," Lucky admitted. "She shouldn't have left me and Abigail to do all the work."

Cora took Lucky's hairbrush off the nightstand. "Friends fight, but friends also forgive. I'm sure you and Pru will work things out." She ran the brush down Lucky's long hair. "But is that the *only* thing bothering you, other than the fact that I won't let you cook all night long?"

"What do you mean?"

"Well, I noticed that you got upset when I mentioned Miss Flores."

Lucky turned around. "Yeah, why did you do that? Dad doesn't need a girlfriend right now. Or ever. Why is everyone pushing this on him? Althea wants him to meet her sister. And Widow Brown wants to make him chicken stew. And now you're trying to get him to marry Miss Flores!"

Cora tucked a strand of hair behind Lucky's ear. "Oh, Lucky, I hope you don't believe I would push your dad into getting married. That is not my intention in the least. He's my brother. I just want him to be happy."

"You're not married. Are you unhappy just because you're not married?"

Cora shook her head. "Of course not. Maybe one day I'll meet a nice gentleman, but for now I am proud to be a single, independent woman." They both looked at the poster on the wall. Milagro's face smiled back at them. "Lucky, things change. Look outside. Last month we were basking in a warm autumn day at the harvest festival, and here we are, surrounded by snow. Seasons change. People change. One day your father might fall in love again."

Lucky frowned. "Or he might not."

"Or he might not." Cora set the hairbrush back on the nightstand. Then she took Lucky's chin in her hand. "But do not be afraid of change. Look how we adapted, you and I. We didn't think we'd ever fit in, but now we're both so busy; we both have friends and meaningful projects. Any changes that come our way, we can face them. Together."

She kissed Lucky's cheek, then turned off the lamp on her way out.

Lucky lay back on the pillow. As the room darkened, her mother's face faded from view. And Lucky was overcome by a desperate feeling. If her dad fell in love, would he forget Lucky's mother? Would he forget what she looked like? How she sounded? The things she said?

Would her mother fade until she disappeared, forever?

22

Lucky gently smacked her alarm clock to stop its buzzing. Then she scrambled out of bed and pulled back the curtains. Though no new snow had fallen, the temperature appeared to have dipped well below freezing. Clusters of icicles hung from the roof's eaves. Was it too cold for the herd to wander in search of food? Poor Spirit. Lucky felt helpless. Why did winter have to be so cruel?

She quickly dressed, then charged downstairs, her sleeves rolled up, ready for work. It wasn't long before Pru and Abigail showed up. "I'm sorry I stormed out," Pru said. "I shouldn't have let Maricela get under my skin."

Any anger Lucky had felt immediately brushed away, like a chalkboard being wiped clean. "I understand," Lucky told her. "Maricela isn't easy to get along with."

"She's stubborn," Abigail said. "Like Señor Carrots."

"Well, I can be just as stubborn," Pru admitted. Lucky and Abigail shared a quick look, for they both knew this was true. Then they all laughed.

No more needed to be said. They were friends, now

and always, and they would finish the project together. But there was so much more to do.

By noon they finished making all the cookies, with no help from Maricela. After bundling into their warmest layers, and passing Cora's inspection, they set out. Lucky carried the burlap bag of cookies, Pru carried a basket of suet cones, and Abigail carried a basket of seed cakes. The herd was their priority, so they headed straight for Pru's barn. But they ran into a big blockade, in the form of Al Granger. "It's too icy to be riding out there," he said. "Can't risk a horse slipping and breaking a leg, or you girls getting hurt."

"But, Dad—"

"I'm not changing my mind about this, Pru, so no use in begging." And off he marched. But a moment later he turned around, real quick. "And don't you go sneaking off. I'm still mad at you girls for almost getting blown up by dynamite. If you go riding, you'll be in a heap of trouble!"

"Drat!" Pru said with a stomp of her foot. "I'm sorry, Lucky."

"It's not your fault the weather's so bad." But Lucky couldn't hide her disappointment. She desperately wanted to give the treats to the mustangs, more than she'd wanted anything in a very long time.

"We can still feed the birds and wild rabbits," Abigail reminded them.

Lucky set the burlap bag down in Pru's barn. They checked on the chickens, bunnies, sheep, goats, Chica Linda, and Boomerang. Everyone seemed happy and warm. Jacques had heated up some water, which they added to the horses' trough to help melt the ice. "Boomerang, look, the water isn't frozen." Abigail cupped her hands into the trough and held up a handful of water. "Come on, Boomerang. See, you can drink it now." Boomerang stuck his nose into her cupped hands and drank. Abigail did this two more times until she had coaxed him to drink from the trough. Meanwhile, Pru grabbed a small stepladder. "So we can reach the higher branches," she explained.

Sounds of laughter and cheers coaxed them in the direction of Pig Pond, which had frozen over thanks to the dip in temperature. The pond was thus named because of its oval shape and because it was in view of Miradero Mel's pen, which happened to be the fanciest pen a pig has ever known—palatial in size and clean as a whistle. That was the kind of accommodation a pig got when he was famous.

Turo and the older students had pulled their ice

skates out of their attics and were taking full advantage of the frozen pond. They'd built a little fire to warm their hands, and they'd set up a metal grill, upon which they were roasting nuts and warming a kettle of cocoa. Parents and younger kids had joined them. "Wow, that looks like fun," Pru said.

"We have work to do," Abigail reminded her.

Maricela did not show up, but they saw her looking out her window as they passed by. She darted behind a curtain when Abigail waved. "Why doesn't she come and help us?" Abigail asked.

"She doesn't *work*, remember?" Pru grumbled.

They knocked on the Gutierrezes' door, but the housekeeper told them that Maricela was busy and wasn't accepting visitors.

"Aunt Cora said something last night," Lucky told Pru and Abigail as they crossed the Gutierrezes' yard. "She said that sometimes, when a person acts mean toward others, that person is actually hurting inside. Do you think Maricela is hurting?"

"I don't see why she'd be hurting," Pru said. They stopped at a walnut tree. While Lucky held the ladder, Pru stood on the top step, hanging a cone from a branch. "She gets everything she wants." That had been Lucky's thought as well, but as she peeked over her shoulder, she caught Maricela looking out the window again. A person who gets everything she wants should look happy. But Maricela looked miserable, a huge frown plastered across her face.

As the PALs made their way through town, they tucked the seed cakes into dry spots beneath shrubs and into rock crevices. Then they hung the last cone in Abigail's yard. Señor Carrots was an expert at standing on his hind legs and stretching his body and neck to snatch things, so they borrowed a taller ladder so they could hang the cone out of the donkey's reach.

By the time their baskets were empty, snow had gotten into their boots and the cold had seeped through their mittens. Pru's house was closest, so they decided to thaw out in her kitchen. Jacques made them big bowls of French onion soup and a platter of buttered toast. While Lucky ate, she couldn't stop thinking about the herd. There was no way Mr. Granger would give them permission to ride if the weather didn't improve.

Just as she sipped her last spoonful of her soup, Turo barged in. "The herd's here," he announced, gasping for breath. His brown hair poked out from under his knit hat. "And there's something you should see!" Lucky's heart skipped a beat. Turo wasn't smiling. He wasn't bringing good news. "Come on," he urged, motioning for them to follow.

Bundled up once again, they hurried outside. The frozen snow crunched beneath their feet as they ran. To make it easier, they stuck to the path of boot prints the older kids had made on their way to Pig Pond. Then they followed Turo past the pond and climbed a small hill. "There!" Turo said, pointing.

The herd stood on the horizon, dark shapes against the snow. They walked with their heads down, searching for food. Lucky counted eighteen horses, plus one foal. Where was the other foal? The herd walked close together, the foal in the middle. Then she noticed two horses far behind the herd. "It's Spirit," Lucky realized. "And one of the foals." Spirit seemed to be walking in a normal manner, only very slowly. The foal, however, was clearly having trouble. It appeared to be staggering. Wobbly on its feet. "Is it hurt?"

"It might be sick," Turo said. "Is it a boy or a girl?"

Pru squinted and stared at the shapes. "We've never seen it up close, so we don't know."

"Look how Spirit is staying with the baby," Abigail said. "He cares."

While it eased Lucky's worry to know that Spirit was watching over the foal, the fact remained that something was wrong. This was terrible news, not just for the foal's sake, but for the entire herd. "If the sick foal is slowing them down, that means they can't walk as far for food. Mrs. Granger said the ability to cover lots of ground is key to the herd's survival in winter."

"You're right," Abigail said. "They're going to need our help."

Pru grabbed Lucky's arm. "We have to change my dad's mind. He has to let us bring food to them."

"But how do we get it to them?" Turo asked. "It's too icy out there for a wagon."

Lucky, Pru, and Abigail looked at one another, then said, "The sleigh!"

23

It wasn't difficult to persuade Pru's mother that the herd needed help. But Al Granger, like his daughter, tended to be a bit stubborn. "I don't see why we should interfere," he said. "Wild critters do just fine on their own. That's the way nature intended it."

"But, Dad, our school project is about helping wild animals," Pru said. "That's the whole point."

"Normally, I would agree with you," Fanny Granger told him. "But these are unusual circumstances. We're dealing with extreme winter weather, the likes of which we rarely see in these parts. And Lucky has a special relationship with this particular herd."

Lucky stood as still as a mountain, holding her breath and waiting for Al's reaction. He remained silent, eyes narrowed, deep in thought. He rubbed his black beard, thinking some more. Then he folded his arms and said assuredly, "I care about the well-being of those mustangs, don't get me wrong, but I still think they know how to fend for themselves."

He wasn't going to help them? Lucky was about to

plead. To beg. But Fanny stepped close to her husband and said, "Al, don't you think it's strange that Spirit has allowed his herd to get so near to town? He knows it's a risk. He knows that you might send out your *mesteñeros*."

Lucky gasped.

"Dad! You wouldn't do that, would you?" Pru cried.

Abigail nearly burst into tears. "No, Mr. Granger, please don't do that. Please don't catch Spirit's herd."

"Hang on, now." Al pushed his hat up his forehead. "I never said I'd do any such thing." This statement was followed by a huge exhale of relief from all three girls. But still, the situation hadn't changed.

"Mrs. Granger is right," Lucky said. "Spirit would never let his herd get this close unless he didn't have a choice. They can't travel because the foal is sick. He could leave the foal behind and let it die to give the rest of the herd a chance, but Spirit isn't doing that." Was Mr. Granger listening to her? Could she convince him? "Spirit is helping the foal and we should help it, too."

Al's expression softened. "I know it's not easy watching something small suffer, but I still say we shouldn't mess with wild critters."

Fanny set her hand on her husband's shoulder. "Need I remind you that your men are the ones who captured Spirit in the first place, thus *messing* with a wild critter?"

Al rubbed the back of his neck. Lucky, Pru, Abigail, Turo, and Fanny warily waited for his response. "Dadburnit, I reckon you're right about that. Okay, we'll take the sleigh out there and drop off a bale of hay."

"And cookies!" Abigail exclaimed. She darted into the barn.

"Cookies?" Al asked.

Pru frowned. "Gee, Dad, haven't you been paying attention to our project? The oatmeal cookies are for the—"

A loud squeal sounded from inside the barn. Everyone ran inside, where they found Abigail holding an empty burlap bag. "Boomerang," she said, shaking a finger at her horse. "You've been very, very bad." Boomerang took a step back and licked his lips, perhaps trying to get rid of the evidence. The chickens pecked gleefully at cookie crumbs that were scattered around Boomerang's feet. Chica Linda tried to look innocent, but the cluster of oats stuck to her nose gave her away.

Lucky groaned. "They ate everything."

"We still have hay," Pru said. "Come on."

"Good luck," Fanny told them.

"Mom, aren't you coming with us?" Pru asked.

"I need to make my rounds," she replied, grabbing her medical bag. "There are other animals that need tending."

"But don't you want to examine the sick foal?" Lucky asked.

"There's no way the herd would let me get close enough," Fanny said. "If the foal is weak from hunger, then the hay will help."

Al, Turo, and the girls removed the tarp and pushed the sleigh to the front of the barn. Aside from cobwebs and peeling paint, it appeared to be in great shape. Like the sleighs in Philadelphia, this one had two bench seats, with the driver's being slightly higher. The cushioning, however, was long gone, having been stolen over the years by field mice for nest-making purposes. But the wooden slats were solid with no signs of rot. The blades formed graceful lines that curved to the front like arching snakes.

They set a bale of hay in the back. Then Al brought

forth his largest horse—a draft horse named Hercules. He was even shaggier than Spirit. He looked like he was wearing furry socks. Turo checked his hooves. "Looks good, Mr. Granger." There wasn't enough room for everyone to go, and Al wanted to limit the weight, so Turo and Abigail volunteered to stay and watch the barn animals.

Lucky and Pru chose the back bench so they could cuddle together against the weather. Al took the front bench. Lucky was surprised by how smoothly the sleigh glided. Hercules seemed to have no trouble pulling it. But they hadn't traveled very far when Al said, "We'll stop here."

"But the herd is still so far away," Lucky said.

"It doesn't matter how far we go, the herd will never let us get close." It was true that as they'd approached, the herd had moved farther away. "And I don't want to make Hercules work too hard in this weather. He's no spring chicken. The mustangs will come get the hay after we leave."

They unloaded the bale and set it on the snow. Al took a knife from his back pocket, removed its leather sheath, then sliced through the cord that had held the bale tight. When the cord snapped, the bale sprung to life, relaxing into a mound and releasing the deep scent of hay. "Those mustangs will smell this. You can count on that," Al said.

Lucky wanted to make sure. She climbed back into the sleigh and stood on the front seat. She put her hands around her mouth and yelled, "Spirit!" He was so far away, and now just a silhouette. She couldn't be certain if he'd heard her. "Spirit! We brought you some food!"

Al returned his knife to its sheath. "You think he understands?"

"Of course he understands," Pru said. "Don't tell Chica Linda I said this, but Spirit is the smartest horse I've ever met."

They all climbed back into the sleigh. "You girls hunker down back there," Al said. "The wind's picking up."

The gust blew across Lucky's face. She and Pru huddled closer. "It's starting to get dark," Lucky said.

"The days are getting shorter," Pru told her.

"Thank you, Mr. Granger," Lucky said. She peered over the back of the sleigh. Had Spirit heard her? Had he smelled the hay?

"No thanks necessary. Let's get you back to a warm

fire." He picked up the reins and, after a sharp whistle, Hercules began pulling them back to town.

Lucky soon lost sight of Spirit and his herd. Then the wind came on so strong, she couldn't watch any longer. She tucked her face into her coat collar.

And she hoped.

24

The voice was faint, but it reached Spirit's ears.
His girl. Why was she calling to him? He wanted to
gallop to her, but the filly was sick and needed his
protection.

He didn't like being this close to town, close to the
men and their ropes. But he remembered a nearby cave
that he'd seen during one of his rides with his girl. It
would be the best place for the herd to stay warm and
dry. His ears pricked with agitation. He felt restless,
alert, searching constantly for anything that might mean
danger.

He watched as his girl headed back to town. The
wind picked up, stinging his nostrils and eyes. But it
carried with it the scent of hay.

His girl had brought hay! Tasty, sweet hay.

Could he lead the herd to the hay, then get them
back to the cave before dark? The filly would make the
going slow. He looked to the sky. Darkness was already
creeping around the mountains. Soon it would be too
cold to stand in the open. He turned toward the pile of
hay, its scent tempting him. His stomach growled. But

then he caught another faint sound. A howl. The foals would be easy prey at night.

They needed to go.

Spirit whinnied at his herd. *Follow me.* He moved to the front and began leading them. Once they were all on the move, he stepped aside and waited for them to pass. Then he took position behind the filly and her mother, matching their pace. The filly stumbled a few times. When she stopped to catch her breath, he gently nudged her with his nose. They had to keep moving. Wolves traveled quickly and the pile of hay would not tempt them. They wanted flesh.

By the time Spirit, the mare, and her filly reached the cave, the rest of the herd was inside, huddled together, their bodies warming the air. They stepped aside, making room for the filly, who crumpled to the ground, exhausted. Spirit licked her face, letting her know that she was safe.

But was she?

He looked into the mare's eyes—eyes they shared, for they'd been born of the same mother. He nuzzled her neck and snorted affectionately.

Sometimes it was this way. Sometimes the young died and there was nothing to be done.

But Spirit wasn't yet ready to give up.

25

Pru Granger invited the girls to her house that
evening to make a second batch of the horse cookies.
She figured that because her kitchen was enormous, with
oversize pots and pans for feeding all the ranch hands,
the three of them would be able to make a larger batch in
a shorter amount of time. And time was of the essence.
Even though they hadn't gotten a close look at the foal,
it was clear that the poor creature was hurting. And
even though it had been a long day of nonstop activity,
the PALs agreed that the herd was more important than
dinner, or sleep, or anything else. If they could do one
thing to help Spirit and his herd, they could provide food.
So that's what they were going to do!

They placed the ingredients on the long kitchen
table. Abigail, being the cookie maker of the group, set
everything in order, starting with the dry ingredients,
followed by the molasses. With Jacques's help they
collected measuring cups and spoons, big mixing bowls,
cookie trays and oven mitts, and a pair of cooling racks.

Jacques handed each girl an apron. "Thanks for
letting us use all of this," Pru told him. Jacques could be

very temperamental about his kitchen, for he kept the pots and pans in spotless condition, oiling the cast-iron skillets to perfection.

"Yeah, we'll clean up our mess, we promise," Lucky said.

He smiled. "You girls have good hearts," he said, picking up his reading glasses and a book. *"Bonne nuit."* Then he retired to his room for the night.

"Isn't Maricela supposed to be doing this project with you?" Fanny asked as she stoked the kitchen stove. "Do you want me to send your father over to her house and pick her up?"

"No thanks," Pru replied. "Maricela made it perfectly clear that she doesn't want to make cookies for horses."

Abigail frowned. "I don't know what Maricela has against horses. Horses are adorable. I just love them!" She set a bowl of apples on the table, then handed a paring knife to Lucky.

"I love horses, too," Fanny said, "but I didn't always feel that way. I didn't like them very much when I was younger." Pru stopped measuring flour and gave her mother a look of disbelief. How was it possible that her mother hadn't liked horses? Her mother loved *all* animals. Fanny reached into the bag of raisins, ate a few, then explained. "I didn't grow up with horses, so when Al and I met, he took me for my first ride. Al was so tall and handsome. I wanted to impress him, so I lied and told him that I had lots of riding experience."

Pru had never heard this story before. She knew that her parents had grown up in very different ways. Her mom had been bookish and more interested in school, while her dad had preferred the outdoors to the classroom. Pru was clearly a combination of both parents. She leaned on the table, eager to hear the rest of the story. The rhythmic *chop chop* of Lucky's knife stopped. Quiet fell over the kitchen.

Fanny continued. "I didn't want Al to think I was scared. He told me that he'd chosen a very gentle mare for me to ride, but she didn't look gentle to me. In fact, when Al wasn't looking, the mare tried to kick me." Fanny laughed. "I think she was jealous."

"Did you tell Mr. Granger that the horse tried to kick you?" Lucky asked.

"No. I was trying to be brave. But I started to worry that the horse would try to throw me off. And whenever Al wasn't looking, she kept nipping at me. So you know what I did?" The girls shook their heads. Fanny grabbed an apple from the bowl. "I gave her a treat. And she loved me after that." She laughed again. "A way to a horse's heart is through her stomach."

"That's really true," Abigail said. "Sometimes I think Boomerang loves food more than he loves me."

Pru pondered her mother's story. Fanny had confessed that she hadn't liked horses because she'd been afraid of them. "Do you think Maricela got scared by a horse?" Pru wondered.

"I already asked her that question," Lucky told them. "She said she isn't afraid. She just doesn't like them."

"I think she doesn't like horses because I like horses," Pru said. "Maricela doesn't like me at all; she never has, and so if I like something, then she will do the opposite. I don't know why, but it's always been that way with her."

"I remember things differently," Fanny said, reaching for more raisins. "When Maricela first moved here, you two were friends."

"What?" Pru cried. Had her mom suddenly gone crazy? "We were *never* friends."

"Yes, you were. Maricela used to walk with you after school. She'd sit right here at this table and have a snack. She often invited you to her house, but you always had riding lessons."

Pru couldn't believe what she was hearing. Maricela?

"If she was my friend, then why didn't she come with me to riding lessons?"

"Her mother wouldn't let her. She said it wasn't ladylike to ride. She was worried Maricela would get hurt."

Was this true? How had Pru forgotten this time in her life? "I...I don't remember."

Fanny wiped her hand on a napkin. "That doesn't surprise me. You were only six. I think Maricela realized that you were busy, so she started playing with Abigail."

"I remember," Abigail said. "We played dress-up in her mom's clothes. And she always had these fancy chocolates to eat." She frowned. "But then we stopped playing. I can't remember why."

Everyone turned to Fanny Granger, waiting for the answer. Fanny smiled gently at her daughter. "Pru is the reason why."

"Me?" Pru said.

"Yes. You invited Abigail to take riding lessons with you. And the two of you became instant best friends. You discovered a shared love of horses."

"I think I get it," Lucky said. "Maricela doesn't like Pru because she thinks she took Abigail away."

"I didn't take her away," Pru insisted. "Not on purpose."

"We know that, sweetie," Fanny said. "But maybe Maricela doesn't know that. You were all so young. It might have felt that way to her."

An image suddenly filled Pru's mind, something that had been buried in the clutter of the past, one of the little things that happen day to day and is swept into a corner. She was sitting at the kitchen table. A girl sat next to her—a girl with auburn curls and a white ribbon. They were eating bread and jam. Both Pru and the girl were laughing.

All of a sudden, it felt to Pru as if she was the bad guy. As if she was being blamed for the fact that she and Abigail had more fun together than with Maricela. "I didn't mean to hurt anyone's feelings," she mumbled.

Lucky moved close to Pru and said very gently, "It's not your fault, Pru. You and Abigail were destined to be friends."

"Yes, we were," Abigail said. "Like peas in a pod."

To Pru's relief, they didn't talk any more about Maricela. This news that they'd once been friends was a bit unsettling. She wanted to think about it. In private.

They set the first batch of cookies into the oven. As they were baking, the girls all took a break around the fire. While they stretched out on the carpet, Fanny sat in an overstuffed armchair and began to peruse the new edition of the *Miradero Gazette*. The front page headline read: "Wolves on the Prowl." There was another article on the page. "Local Donkey Runs Amok," with a photo of Snips chasing Señor Carrots through the train station.

"Mrs. Granger?" Lucky asked. "What's going to happen to the foal?"

Fanny looked up from her reading. "You said it was limping?"

"It was walking very slowly," Lucky said.

"Boomerang walks like that when he doesn't want to go back to the barn," Abigail said.

Fanny thought a moment. "Well, if the foal was having trouble walking, it could be a lot of things. Dehydration can be an issue this time of year, and that causes fatigue. The foal might be weak from an infection. There are so many things that could make a horse feel bad—colic, parasites. I wouldn't know without conducting an examination." She set the paper on her lap. "You'll have to face the fact that the foal might die."

Pru knew this was true. Life on a ranch had taught her all about the circle of life. If an animal was too weak, it died. If strong, it lived. Sometimes her mother could help with medicine, sometimes she couldn't. Pru remembered when one of their foals had died only three hours after being born. The foal had been born too early and just didn't have the strength to make it. "We don't even know if it's a boy or a girl," she realized.

Lucky sighed. "I hope it doesn't die."

"As do we all," Fanny said.

Al Granger strode in. "What's with all the gloomy faces?"

Pru scrambled to her feet. "Dad, will you help us deliver the horse cookies in the morning? We want to take them out to the herd."

"What? More food for the herd? I thought…" He caught the hopeful look on Lucky's face. "Yes, of course. We'll hitch up the sleigh at first light."

Pru threw her arms around his waist. "Thanks, Dad."

"Yes, thank you, Mr. Granger," Lucky said.

While Al escorted Lucky and Abigail home, Pru went down to the barn for her evening check on the animals. Everyone seemed content. The rabbits had burrowed beneath a pile of straw. The chickens were fast asleep in their nests. Chica Linda and Boomerang nodded at Pru, but made no noise, as if they didn't want to wake the others. Pru leaned over one of the stall doors and gazed down at the sheep and goats, who were contentedly huddled together. She thought about the wild birds and wild rabbits who would sleep that night with full bellies, thanks to all the work she, Abigail, and Lucky had done. Maricela was missing out on something important.

Maricela, who'd once been her friend.

Part Four

26

The next morning, Lucky headed to the Grangers' at dawn. Both Jim and Cora knew she was going to deliver the horse cookies today, and she'd assured them that Pru's father would be helping. She hoped the herd had eaten the hay and that they'd slept well, with full bellies. But mostly, she hoped that the foal was feeling better. Maybe she could persuade Al to deliver a second bale along with the cookies. Couldn't hurt to try.

There was no sign of Spirit along the way. She kept her eyes peeled for a flash of buckskin, her ears alert for his neigh. Snow crunched beneath her boots. Her nose started to sting, so she pulled up her scarf. When she arrived at Pru's house, Abigail was already there. They put the horse cookies into a burlap bag and hurried down to the barn to find Al. But they were greeted with bad news.

"The weather's gonna take a turn for the worse," Al said, pointing into the distance where ominous, dark clouds hung over the flattop mountains. "We're in for a blizzard."

"How do you know?" Lucky asked.

"Well, the temperature got colder and the humidity

got higher. You feel that wind? When it picks up, it'll be one mess of a storm. Seen a few blizzards in my life. They can take a while to develop, and I'm guessing we'll be in for it tonight. But you never know. The wind could pick up earlier. I don't want to get caught out there. When a blizzard hits, no one, critter or person, can see through it. The cookie delivery will have to wait."

"But—" Pru started to object, but her father gave her a don't-argue-with-me look. "Yeah, okay," she said, her shoulders deflating.

As Mr. Granger set out to do morning chores, the girls headed into the barn, where they were greeted with clucks, bleats, and neighs. "Hello, Licorice. Hello, Zebra and Corncob and Cherry and Reddy," Abigail said.

"You remember those aren't their real names, right?" Pru teased.

"They're nicknames," Abigail said. "Oh, I forgot to name the sheep. Hello, Woolly and Fluffy and—"

Though Abigail's cheerfulness was usually infectious, frustration welled in Lucky's chest. "I wish winter would just be over!" she interrupted, with a stomp of her boot. "This stupid weather keeps getting in our way!" Lucky kicked a bucket, then slumped onto a bench, her arms tightly folded. Abigail and Pru shared a wide-eyed look, but neither told Lucky to calm down. Her frustration was totally understandable.

Pru grabbed a rake and began to break up the ice in the trough. "As soon as the blizzard passes through, we'll go out there and deliver the cookies."

"This time I won't let Boomerang eat them," Abigail said, setting the burlap bag into a cupboard. "I promise!"

A loud neigh filled the air. "Spirit!" Lucky cried, jumping to her feet. He'd entered through the swinging door in his stall. He neighed again and his ears flicked back and forth. "Spirit, what's wrong?" He began to pace, his ears continuing to flicker. "He's sweating."

"He's anxious," Pru told her. "What's up, boy?"

Spirit neighed again, so loudly that the chickens squawked and the bunnies scurried behind a hay bale. He turned around and quickly headed back through the door. Lucky, Pru, and Abigail followed. Outside, Spirit continued pacing, looking toward the mountains. Then he stuck his nose under Lucky's hand. She frowned at him and shook her head. "I can't ride today. A blizzard might be coming." But he wouldn't stop pushing at her, in a way he'd never done before. At first the nudges were gentle, but they turned insistent. "He's trying to tell me something. Do you think it's about the foal? Do you think it needs our help?"

Lucky nearly lost her balance when Spirit pushed her again. "He's acting so weird," Abigail said.

Pru put her hands on her hips. "I think he wants to show you something." Spirit neighed again. Chica Linda and Boomerang also neighed, as if in agreement.

A familiar feeling took over Lucky's body. Instinct. She'd had this sensation once before, when Pru and Abigail had ridden into the canyon, unaware that the railroad workers were going to dynamite so they could lay new tracks. Without knowing what would happen, Lucky had climbed onto Spirit's back and asked for his help. She'd put her trust in him then, but now he was asking for her help. She grabbed his mane and pulled herself onto his back.

Abigail gasped. "Lucky?" She turned to Pru. "Do you see what … Uh-oh. I know that look on your face. Pru, you're going to get into so much trouble!" Pru was already reaching for her saddle.

"I'd rather get into trouble than let that foal die," Pru said. "Chica Linda is strong. She can help us."

"Well, if you're going, then I'm going!" Abigail announced.

Lucky wanted to hug her friends, but there was no

time to spare. "Abigail, would you stay here? If we all disappear, our parents will get worried. But if you stay…"

"You want me to lie?" Abigail scrunched up her face, as if a live bug had flown into her mouth.

"No, we're not asking you to lie," Lucky replied. "I just think we can buy some time if you stay. Maybe it will take everyone longer to realize Pru and I are gone if you're still here."

"Fine," Abigail said, though she didn't sound too happy about it. She ran to the cupboard. "Don't forget these." She handed the cookie-filled bag to Lucky. Lucky tucked the bag under her coat, then clutched Spirit's mane with both hands. "Be careful!" Abigail called as Lucky and Pru rode away.

"We need to keep our eyes on those clouds," Pru hollered as they rode. "If they start to move this way, we have to turn right around."

"Agreed!"

No new snow had fallen, thus the sleigh's tracks from yesterday were still visible and made an easier path for the horses to traverse. The dark clouds, ominous on the horizon, seemed content to stay where they were. When the girls reached the pile of hay, Lucky tugged on Spirit's mane and called, "Whoa!" Both he and Chica Linda halted. Lucky looked down. "They didn't eat anything," she said, her voice heavy with disappointment.

"It's frozen solid," Pru noted. "They can't eat it now."

Spirit didn't want to stop moving. He pushed forward, without waiting for Lucky's command. They continued to head east, toward Pitchfork Canyon. As they rode, Lucky tried not to think about how angry their parents would be when they found out about this ride. *If* they found out. Abigail would do her best to cover for them, but would she be able to? Lucky wasn't sure. Hopefully she and Pru would get back to the barn before anyone noticed they were gone. But if they did get caught, Lucky would accept whatever punishment was doled out. Better to have months of chores, knowing that they'd tried to help the foal.

Miradero disappeared from view, and a few minutes later, Lucky and Pru reached the canyon. Spirit led them around an outcropping of rock. As they turned the corner, Lucky took a sharp, surprised breath. The herd stood right in front of her! She'd never seen them this close. They were so beautiful! Two of the mustangs were solid black; others were mixtures of chocolates and tans and some had white splotches, but they were all as shaggy as Spirit.

At the sound of Spirit's arrival, the mustangs lifted their heads. Eyes widened when they spied Lucky on his back. A moment later, Chica Linda and Pru appeared. Agitation rolled over the mustangs, like a wave across sand. Their bodies stiffened, ears flicked. They began to turn, readying themselves to run. But Spirit neighed at them. They listened, and calm returned. Spirit snorted at Chica Linda, who came to a full stop. It appeared he wanted her to wait. "We'll stay here," Pru whispered.

With Lucky still on his back, Spirit began to walk through the herd. The mustangs stepped aside, making room for him. She could have reached out and touched them as she passed by, but she didn't. They were allowing her into their world. She wanted to be respectful, but her hands twitched, almost as if they had a mind of their own. Oh, how she wanted to pet all of them.

She noticed that, aside from a few spindly trees, the area was lacking in vegetation. The ground appeared frozen solid and icicles hung from crevices in the rocks. There was nothing to eat here. A black stallion stepped forward. He and Spirit greeted each other. Then the stallion sniffed Lucky's leg. She held very still. He was a wild creature, after all, and fear could cause him to bite her. He sniffed her boot, then shook his head as if he didn't like what he'd smelled. Who could blame him for not trusting people? He'd probably watched the *mesteñeros* when they'd captured Spirit. But then his nose found the bag under Lucky's coat.

The cookies.

This was the perfect opportunity to feed the herd. Lucky unbuttoned her coat and pulled out the bag. Heads immediately turned as oat and apple scents filled the air. She didn't want to risk losing a finger, so she dropped a cookie at the black stallion's feet. He ate it without hesitation. As Spirit resumed walking, Lucky dropped the cookies, one by one, onto the ground. They were gobbled up so quickly, it looked as if they'd been inhaled. Lucky smiled. Abigail would be so happy to hear that the mustangs loved her treats.

"Do you see the foal?" Pru called, keeping her voice as quiet as possible.

Lucky looked over her shoulder and shook her head. Where was the sick foal? Her stomach tightened. Had it already perished? She dropped a few more cookies, and then Spirit stopped walking. A brown-and-white horse stepped aside, revealing an entrance to a cave. The opening was plenty large for horses. Another horse stepped out of the cave: a buckskin mare with a white splotch on her nose that matched Spirit's. Was she his sister? Spirit and the mare nuzzled, and then she moved aside, allowing Spirit to carry Lucky into the cave. Lucky ducked, so as not to hit her head on the opening. It was dark in there. Spirit stopped moving. Lucky heard the foal before she saw it.

It was breathing as if every breath hurt.

27

Lucky slid off Spirit's back and stumbled forward, her eyes still adjusting to the dim light. A shape lay in front of her. It was the foal, lying on its side. At the sound of Lucky's boots, it raised its head. "Don't be afraid," Lucky said softly. "I won't hurt you." She took a few steps forward.

Alarmed by Lucky's presence, the foal tried to get to its feet, but it was clearly a struggle. It groaned, unable to muster the strength to escape. Spirit moved in front of Lucky and pressed his nose against the foal's cheek. The foal calmed and stopped struggling. Then Spirit stepped aside. Even though the mare was watching intently, she also stepped aside. It seemed to Lucky that the horses had given her permission to approach. She continued to speak in hushed tones. "I just want to look at you," she said as she knelt beside it. *I wish Mrs. Granger were here*, she thought. *And Pru, too.* Lucky wasn't really sure what she was searching for. Signs of injury? Her eyes had fully adjusted now and her gaze traveled over the foal's body. No signs of blood, no cuts or gashes. But something did look different. Its belly seemed bloated. And that's when Lucky noticed that the foal was a filly.

"Hello, sweet thing," she said. She reached into the bag and offered an oatmeal cookie. The filly sniffed it, then turned away. Her eyelids seemed heavy, as if she were having trouble staying awake. "Poor girl," Lucky whispered, but she didn't reach out to touch her because she didn't want to upset the filly's mother.

Lucky got to her feet and hurried outside. The herd parted as she ran toward Pru and Chica Linda. Pru dismounted. "What happened?"

"It's a filly," Lucky explained. "She's still alive but she's very sick. Her belly is swollen and she seems really tired, like she has no energy. She couldn't even get to her feet. And she wouldn't eat the cookie."

Pru frowned. "When a horse won't eat, that's a very bad sign."

Lucky began to pace in a frantic way. Chica Linda and Pru didn't take their eyes off her, as if watching a tennis match. "Spirit came to get me because he needs our help. I'm sure of it. Otherwise he would never have brought us to his herd. I thought maybe the foal just needed food. But I was wrong." There was only one thing to do. Lucky came to a dead stop. "We need your mom."

"You're right. Let's ride back and tell her what we've found." Pru stuck her foot into the stirrup and pulled herself into the saddle. Then she reached a hand out to Lucky. "Come on. Let's go."

Lucky hesitated. She looked back at the cave. "I'm staying here," she said.

"What? Are you crazy? I can't leave you out here alone. Come on. We'll talk to my mom. She'll know what to do."

Lucky looked up at Pru. Surely she'd understand. "Spirit trusts me. He came to get me. I need to stay here. The filly is too weak to walk to the river, so I'm going to try to melt some snow and get her to drink. Your mom said that dehydration was one of the biggest dangers the herd would face in the winter."

Pru shook her head. "I don't like this, Lucky. If I leave you out here, it's not right. What if the blizzard comes?"

"It won't." Lucky looked to the mountains. The clouds had not moved closer, nor had the wind picked up. "Listen to me, Pru. If I ride back with you, and we tell your parents what we discovered, there's no way they'll let us come back. Your dad is too worried about the weather. And he'll say that we should just let nature take its course with the filly. But if I stay out here, then they'll have to ride this way, because they'll have to come and get me."

"That's brilliant," Pru said. "But they won't be happy. And we'll get into a ton of trouble."

"I know we will. But we accepted that fate when we rode out here." She waited for a decision. Pru, the adventurer, the risk taker, the true friend. Pru wouldn't fail her.

Pru grabbed the reins. "Stay safe. I'll be right back!" With an energetic neigh, Chica Linda took off toward Miradero.

Lucky didn't waste any time. Somehow she needed to get water to the filly. But it was too far to walk to the river. What could she do? Then she remembered how Abigail had held water in her hands for Boomerang to drink. That would work. But she'd first have to melt snow. How? What could she use as a container? Did she have anything that could hold water? She checked her pockets, thought about her hat for a moment, then gazed down at her boots. They were waterproof.

With gloves on, she scooped an armful of snow and carried it into the cave. The herd watched warily, but they seemed to have accepted her presence, for they allowed her to walk between them. She dumped the snow onto the cave floor, then went outside for another armful, repeating the process until she had a good-size pile. Then, back inside, she took off her right boot and began to pack it with snow. Under normal circumstances, drinking boot water wouldn't be anyone's first choice, but this was an emergency. And didn't horses drink from all sorts of places, including mud puddles?

Spirit watched Lucky, his ears pinned forward with curiosity. He sniffed her bare sock and looked at her as if to say, *What in the world are you doing?* The mare stood by his side, her brown eyes still following Lucky's every move. *Poor mama*, Lucky thought. *How worried she must be.*

Lucky looked into the boot. "How am I going to melt this?" she asked out loud. Spirit snorted, his warm breath blowing across Lucky's face. Of course! She'd been around horses long enough to know that they exuded warmth. So she took her boot and tucked it into the filly's front leg resting it against her chest. The filly was too weak to protest. Her head fell back to the ground. *Melt,* Lucky thought. *Hurry up and melt!*

It seemed to take forever, but eventually the snow level began to recede. The herd packed tightly together, which helped block some of the chilly winter wind. Lucky shook the boot. Water sloshed at the bottom. She took off her gloves and tucked them into her pocket. Then she scooted close to the filly's head. She took off her coat and wadded it into a ball, then tucked it under the filly's cheek, trying to raise her head off the ground as much as possible. "It's okay, girl," she kept cooing. Then, with her left hand cupped, she poured the water from her boot until it filled her palm. "I know you'd rather drink out of a river or a nice, fresh lake, but this boot will have to do." She pressed her palm against the filly's mouth. She didn't respond. Lucky tilted her hand so some water dripped onto the filly's lips. She opened her mouth. Yes! She lapped at the water. Another handful, then another, again and again until the boot was empty.

Lucky was about to scoop more snow into her boot and start the process again when the cave suddenly went dark. She ran to the entrance. The wind had picked up, howling between the rocks. Snow swirled as if the world outside the cave had been shaken like a snow globe. Trying to flee the bitter wind, the mustangs pushed past Lucky and squeezed into the cave. Even they knew something bad was brewing. For the first time since Pru had left, fear gripped Lucky's entire body.

The blizzard had arrived.

28

Spirit followed Lucky out of the cave. The sky had turned dark. Wind howled, whipping around trees and between canyon walls. Snow fell from the sky and rose from the ground, swirling in a wall of whiteness. Spirit pressed up against Lucky, to let her know that he was there. He nudged her, trying to coax her back into the cave with his herd.

A branch cracked. With a lunge, Spirit pushed Lucky aside just in time. The tree limb landed in the snow where she'd been standing. She regained her balance, then threw her arms around his neck. Another gust of wind screamed. Lucky let go and they both darted into the cave.

The herd settled, some lying down, others standing, closing their eyes. Spirit knew they would sleep well tonight, for their stomachs did not ache, thanks to the treats Lucky had brought.

"She needs more water," Lucky said. She sat beside the filly and offered water from her hands. But, despite Lucky's efforts, the filly was not getting better. Spirit nudged her again and again. Drink more. Drink more.

Lucky was shivering. He ran his nose over her hands. They were cold, like ice. He sniffed her foot. It was wet without the boot. Lucky's lips were blue, her jaw trembling. He needed to keep her warm.

The storm raged outside, as if the wind were angry. But inside the cave, the air warmed with the heat and breath of Spirit's herd. Spirit lay down. Lucky tucked up next to him. And soon, his girl stopped shivering.

29

Something was licking her face.

"Stop it," Lucky grumbled, her eyes closed. She wiped her face, then rolled onto her side. Her pillow felt different. Furry. From very far away, someone called her name. *Lucky! Lucky!* But there were no dream images to go along with the voice. Something licked her face again. She sat up, eyes flying open. A huge pair of brown eyes stared at her. "Spirit?" Then she remembered. She was in a cave. Night had passed. Was it morning already? She turned, fearful of what she'd find. But then she sighed with relief. The filly was still there and she was still breathing. The mare lay beside her. But where was the rest of the herd?

Lucky grabbed her boot and pulled it onto her foot. Then she scrambled to her feet. Her legs were cramped, so she stumbled as she made her way to the cave's opening. Her palms felt raw, almost as if they'd been burned. But that didn't matter. The filly was still alive, so there was a chance she could be saved.

Calm had settled over the canyon, accompanied by the soft light of dawn. With no wind, the air felt warmer than it had in weeks. The herd had already left to look for food and water, their hoofprints visible in the snow that the blizzard had dumped overnight.

"Lucky!"

"Dad!"

Jim threw himself off his horse and ran toward Lucky, his arms outstretched. Then he clasped her to his chest and squeezed so hard she couldn't breathe. "Lucky," he said, his voice cracking. Was he choking back tears? "Lucky," he repeated. "I couldn't get to you. I tried. Believe me, I tried!"

"Dad, I'm okay."

He held her at arm's length, his eyes wild with fear. "Are you certain you're okay? Are you certain?"

"Yes," she said. He sighed with relief, and for a brief moment, he seemed as calm as the morning itself. But then the look in his eyes changed, igniting like a firecracker. "How could you do this? Staying out here by yourself? Do you know how worried we've been? Your aunt is beside herself! We couldn't get to you! Do you—" Then he hugged her again. "I don't know what I would do if I ever lost you," he said. This time, he didn't try to hold back the tears. Nor did she. It nearly broke her heart knowing that she'd made her father cry.

"Dad, I'm okay. Really, I am. I'm sorry that I upset you and Aunt Cora."

"You upset everyone!" Al Granger said as he pulled Hercules to a stop. Fanny sat beside him in the sleigh. Pru and Abigail were on Chica Linda and Boomerang. And three of the ranch hands had joined them as well, riding on Granger horses. Pru and Abigail dismounted and ran to Lucky's side. There were hugs all around. Even Al Granger hugged her. "We're all relieved to find you, Lucky. That was quite the night. We thought we were going to lose your dad, too."

Lucky looked at Jim. "What's he talking about?"

"I tried to find you," Jim explained. "I couldn't stand just waiting. I had to look for you. But it was impossible to see through the blizzard. I got lost almost immediately. Al found me and led me back."

"Lucky, why are your hands so red?" Abigail asked.

Jim scowled. "Where are your gloves?"

"They got wet, from scooping snow. It's a long story."

Lucky knew she needed to apologize, and that, perhaps, she'd be apologizing for the rest of her life. But that would have to wait. "Mrs. Granger," she called. She ran up to the sleigh. "The filly needs you. She's going to die."

Fanny Granger grabbed her black bag and jumped out of the sleigh. "Show me," she said. Everyone began to follow Lucky toward the cave. But Spirit blocked the cave's opening. He lowered his head and glared at Al and the ranch hands. Who could blame him? Earlier that year they'd tried to break him. Spirit stomped a hoof. They all took a step back.

"Spirit is being protective," Lucky explained. "The filly and her mom will get scared if we all go inside."

"We'll wait here," Pru told her.

Lucky motioned to Fanny. "Come on. Spirit will let you in." Lucky and Fanny walked past Spirit. Once inside, Fanny set her medical bag on the ground, then knelt next to the filly. The mare got to her feet and began to pace. Fanny gently pulled back the filly's eyelids and looked into her eyes. She felt the filly's neck and shoulders. She ran her hands down the legs. Then she took a stethoscope from her bag and listened to her heart. She next pressed the stethoscope against her belly. The filly moaned. "Colic," Fanny said.

"What's that?" Lucky asked.

"People sometimes call it 'fret.' It's like a really bad bellyache. None of the other mustangs are ill, is that correct?" Lucky nodded. "I'm guessing that, because of the dwindling food sources, this filly ate something she wasn't supposed to eat. And as the pain increased, she stopped eating and stopped drinking. She's dangerously dehydrated."

"I tried giving her water last night. She drank about a half a boot full. But it's difficult to know for certain. Some of the water dripped onto the ground."

Fanny raised an eyebrow. "You used your boot? How ingenious," she said, clearly impressed.

Then came the question Lucky dreaded asking. "Can you save her?"

Fanny tucked the stethoscope back into her bag. "It might be too late, but I'm willing to try if you are."

"Of course," Lucky said.

"Then let's get her back to the ramada."

The mare wasn't going to like what they were about to do. If only Lucky could explain to her that they needed to take her baby away or else she would die. But even more concerning was that Lucky would need to persuade Spirit to step aside and let Al and his men into the cave. Lucky ran her hand along Spirit's mane. "You've got to trust me," she told him. "You brought me out here and now I'm going to help, but we need to take the filly back to town. These men won't hurt her." Spirit would not budge.

"We could rope him," Earl, one of the ranch hands, suggested. "We could make him step aside."

"No!" Lucky glared at Earl. "No one will ever put ropes on Spirit. Never again." She gave Spirit a gentle push. Then a shove. "Spirit, move!" But he stood firmly in place, his gaze never leaving Al.

"Dad, he doesn't like you," Pru said.

"He remembers me, that's for certain," Al said. "I still got a sore spot from when he threw me out of the corral."

Lucky realized what had to be done.

"Mr. Granger, you've got to talk to him. He doesn't trust you."

"Talk to him?" He scratched his beard.

"Al!" Fanny called from the cave. "We need you and your men to move the filly onto the sleigh. So talk to the dang horse!"

"Fine." Al walked slowly toward Spirit, his hand outstretched, palm facing up, the way one does to a dog. "That's a good boy," he said. Spirit's ears pinned back. "I'm not gonna hurt you. We just want to help that little filly." Spirit tossed his head. Then he pulled back his lips and sneered. Al stopped walking.

"He's gonna bite!"

Lucky stepped between Spirit and Al. She reached out and took Spirit's face in her hands. "Please," she said to him. "Please trust me." Spirit's ears relaxed. His nostrils vibrated as he released a slow breath. This time, when Lucky gently pushed him, he stepped aside.

While Lucky continued to keep Spirit calm, Al spread a blanket on the cave floor. Then, working together, Al, Jim, Pru, Abigail, and the ranch hands carefully lifted and set the filly onto the blanket. The mare paced nervously. "One, two, three," Al said, and holding the edges of the blanket, they lifted and carried her to the sleigh. Earl had removed the back of the sleigh and the back seat so they could set the filly inside.

Fanny climbed in and laid a blanket over her. "Let's go," she told her husband. Al took the reins and the sleigh began its journey back home. The mare followed.

While Jim mounted his horse, Lucky pulled herself onto Spirit's back. "Dad, I'm sorry," she said as they rode side by side. "I'm sorry for making you worry about me."

"You see how that mare is following the sleigh?" Jim asked. Lucky nodded. "She won't let her baby out of her sight. That's how I feel, every day, about you. But when I do let you go off, I trust you to make the right decisions. Staying by yourself, out here in the canyon, with a storm approaching, was not the right decision."

"Dad—"

"We'll talk about it at home." Lucky cringed. She couldn't remember her father ever being this upset with her—not even when she'd barely escaped the dynamite in Filbert Canyon.

They spoke not another word the entire ride back.

30

It looked as if the entire population of Miradero was waiting at the Granger Ramada, but the first face Lucky saw was her aunt's. Cora gripped her skirt and ran straight at Spirit. He skidded to a stop, unsure about the bundle of energy careening toward him. The moment Lucky slid to the ground, she found herself in her aunt's arms. "Lucky, Lucky, Lucky," Cora kept saying, over and over. Lucky didn't squirm to get away. "Lucky, oh my darling Lucky," Cora sobbed. Dark circles clung beneath Cora's eyes and her usually perfect bun was loose, with layers of hair falling around her face.

Jim spoke gently to his sister. "She's fine, Cora. She's not hurt."

"Are you sure you're fine?" Cora asked, now holding Lucky at arm's length. "Did you get hypothermia? Did you get frostbite?" She pressed her palm against Lucky's forehead. "Oh, why didn't you wear more layers? I'm always telling you to wear more layers!" Lucky didn't want to tell Cora about her sore hands, so she hid them in her pockets.

"I'm fine; really, I am."

Like Jim had before, Cora's expression turned fierce. "Well, you're in big trouble, young lady!"

"I know."

Cora's anger quickly melted into relief and gratitude. "Oh, thank goodness you're back home." Jim handed Cora his handkerchief.

Lucky hugged Cora again, fully aware that she'd now made her father *and* her aunt cry. "I didn't mean to be gone so long," she tried to explain. "I'm sorry."

As others began to gather around, Spirit and the mare retreated to a nearby hill. Neither wanted to be so close to that many people, especially the one who was wailing.

Mayor Gutierrez stepped forward. "What a lovely and touching family reunion," he said. Then he put his arm around Lucky's shoulder and posed as the *Miradero Gazette*'s photographer took a picture. "Lucky, on behalf of the entire town, I'd like to welcome you back and say that we are all relieved you are safe and sound." He spoke as he always did, as if giving a speech.

Althea was there, along with a group of women from the Miradero Ladies' Aid Society. "Lucky, you worried us sick. I thought I was going to have to hog-tie your aunt. She plumb went out of her mind with worry."

"Sorry," Lucky said.

Even Miss Flores was there, along with Turo, Snips, and the rest of Lucky's classmates. "Lucky, we are so happy you're safe," Miss Flores said.

Lucky realized it was Monday. "Why aren't you in school?" she wondered.

Miss Flores looked puzzled. "School? How could we possibly think about learning with you missing?"

"We were all getting ready to help with the search," Turo explained.

Lucky swallowed hard, holding back tears. All these people had been worried about her. They all cared. And it wasn't just the school that had closed—Winthrop was there, so that meant the general store wasn't open, either. She recognized shopkeepers, Tanglefoot Inn staff, and even Miradero Mel's owner. This little town had come to a standstill for her. She might have started crying, too, but there was a pressing matter to attend to. She cupped her hands around her mouth. "Everyone!" she called. "I'm very, very sorry that I caused so much worry. And I want to thank each one of you in person, and I will, but right now, I need to help Mrs. Granger."

As the crowd began to drift back to their homes, Lucky hurried into the barn. The farmhands had carried the filly inside. According to Fanny, they needed to get her hydrated and give her some medicine to settle her stomach. Jacques brewed a special herbal tea, which Fanny had successfully used on other horses. He flavored it with apple juice to make it more appealing, for horses love the scent and flavor of apples. Once it cooled, Lucky hand-fed it to the filly. This was a slow process, but Lucky knew they needed to get as much liquid into her as possible.

"Her mom is still waiting outside," Abigail said. "She looks a looks a lot like Spirit. Do you think she's his sister?"

Lucky nodded. "That's my guess."

With the feeding under way, Fanny, Al, Jim, Cora, Miss Flores, and Althea walked up to the Grangers' kitchen for a hearty breakfast. All that worrying about Lucky had left them famished. The PALs insisted on staying in the barn.

"You really scared us," Pru said as soon as the others had left.

"Even Boomerang was worried," Abigail told her. "Isn't that right, Boomerang?" He stepped forward and before Lucky could duck out of the way, he licked her face.

"Uh, thanks, Boomerang," she said, wiping away the slobber with her sleeve. "I love you, too."

"I think we should make a pact," Pru said. "That we never, ever leave one of us alone like that again. That we always stick together!" That was an easy pact to agree to, and so they did.

While Pru and Abigail tended to the other critters, Lucky didn't leave the filly's side. Jacques brought more medicinal tea and ham sandwiches for the girls. Before they took a break to eat, Pru and Abigail carried some hay and a bucket of water to the hill and fed Spirit and the mare.

"I see you're back." The snide voice belonged to the one and only Maricela. As she entered the barn, Chica Linda and Boomerang turned their rumps to her. "My mom said you'd probably get eaten by wolves." She paused, looking down at her feet. "I'm glad you didn't get eaten by wolves."

"Gee, I think that's the nicest thing I've ever heard you say," Pru told her.

Maricela ignored Pru and instead walked up to the stall. "What's everyone looking at?"

Lucky put her finger to her lip. "Try to be as quiet as possible," she whispered. "We don't want to upset her."

"Upset who?" Maricela asked as she peered over the stall door.

"That's the horse Lucky saved," Pru told her.

"It wasn't just me. It was everyone who saved her," Lucky said.

"But you risked your life," Abigail said. "You're a hero."

Lucky sighed. "I'm not a hero. We did this together. Besides, I didn't risk my life. Spirit was with me. He kept me warm and he would have taken me home after the blizzard had passed."

"Well, I think you're a hero," Pru said. "Not just because you wanted to save a horse, but because you worked so hard on our *group project*." She narrowed her eyes at Maricela. "When your *co-leader* did nothing, you got up early and stayed up late to finish the work so we wouldn't fail. I think that's heroic. What do you think, *Maricela*?"

Maricela didn't seem to be listening. She took a step into the stall. Then another. "Is he going to die?" she asked.

"It's a she," Lucky said. "A filly. And we're not sure if she's going to die. She might." Lucky looked down at the little face. The filly's eyes were closed, her breathing steady. Every once in a while her eyelids twitched. Was she dreaming? If so, what did horses dream about? Probably warm spring days, with soft green grass and butterflies to chase. *Those days will be here soon*, Lucky thought. *Just hold on and you'll see them again.*

Maricela took another step. Wait. Was she actually walking toward a horse? Lucky, Pru, and Abigail all watched, their expressions wide with wonder, as Maricela knelt in the straw, reached out, and ever so gently touched the filly's shoulder. "She's so soft. I've never pet a baby horse. How old is she?"

"We think about six months," Lucky said.

"We think she's Spirit's niece," Abigail added.

At the touch, the filly opened her eyes, lifted her head, and gazed at Maricela. "She's so cute," Maricela cooed. "She has such pretty long eyelashes." Then she leaned over and delicately kissed the filly's cheek. Silence fell over the barn. Even the chickens stopped scratching. At that moment, the only thing that could have surprised Lucky more was if Maricela had planted a kiss on Pru's cheek.

"You want to give her some medicine?" Lucky asked.

"Can I?"

What was happening? Not only was Maricela cooing over a horse, she wanted to help? Lucky showed her how to hand-feed the filly and she did it. With no complaints. Her fancy wool coat was getting dirty and she didn't seem to care. "She's the sweetest horse I've ever seen. Can I keep her? Can she be mine?"

"Maricela, we thought you didn't like horses," Abigail said.

"Why would you ever think that?" Maricela asked.

"Why?" Pru blurted out. "Because you're always calling them smelly and stupid. And you didn't want our group project to have anything to do with horses. That's why."

Maricela shrugged. "Well, maybe I don't like *some* horses." She quickly glanced at Chica Linda and Boomerang.

Abigail frowned. "How could you not like Boomerang? He's never done anything mean to anybody. Ever. And he can't help it if he gets gassy. He eats too much."

"I think I know why," Lucky said. Maricela stopped feeding the filly. She straightened her back and shoulders, as if readying herself to take whatever punch Lucky was about to give. But this wasn't a punch. Lucky had been thinking a lot about the situation, and it was time to straighten this out. Lucky looked at Pru and Abigail. "It's not because they are horses. It's because they are *your* horses." She paused to let it sink in.

"Maricela doesn't like your horses because she believes that they kept you from being her friend."

Abigail frowned. "I don't understand."

Suddenly, Maricela's eyes welled with tears. Lucky hadn't expected that reaction. She thought that Maricela would deny everything. Or would stomp away in a huff. But her shoulders sank, and when she spoke, her voice was so quiet they all had to lean forward to hear. "Pru was too busy to be my friend, so I became friends with Abigail. We were having so much fun together. We had tea parties; we colored pictures; we played dress-up." She looked at Pru. "But then you told Abigail all about your riding lessons. You took her away from me."

"No I didn't," Pru said.

"Yes you did." Maricela wiped a tear off her cheek. "Abigail started riding with you every day. There was no time for me."

"Gosh, Maricela, Pru didn't take me away. I found out that I loved riding, and then I got Boomerang and, well, horses are a ton of work. You have to groom them, feed them, exercise them, play with them, talk to them, and sing to them. Boomerang loves it when I sing. All of that takes a lot of time."

Pru leaned against the stall. "Is that why you're

always mad at me? You think I took Abigail away on purpose?"

"Yes," Maricela said, her tears now gone. She held out her chin in a look of defiance.

Both Lucky and Abigail stayed quiet. This was a moment that needed to happen. Pru and Maricela had been fighting a battle and they needed to tell each other how they felt.

"Is that why you ruined my audition?" Pru asked, hands on hips. Maricela looked away. "I knew it! You changed the music so I'd be off-key and sound horrible. Why would you do something like that?"

Maricela slowly got to her feet. Then she carefully stepped past the filly until she stood face-to-face with Pru. Lucky and Abigail held perfectly still, though Lucky was ready to throw herself between them should words turns into actual punches. "Maybe I did swap the alto sheet music for soprano sheet music. I know you can't hit those high notes. And maybe I did take my dad's key and sneak into Town Hall and throw away your Founder's Day speech, but—" Maricela gasped, as if surprised by her own words. Had she confessed more than she'd intended? "But you deserved it, for being mean to me."

"I was never mean to you."

Tears welled again. "Everyone likes you. Everyone is your friend. And then Lucky came to town and I tried really hard to be Lucky's friend, but you took her away, too. You all started riding together. Once again, I lost out to a stupid horse."

Lucky wanted to point out that she'd met Spirit without Pru's help, but she continued to keep quiet. For a long time now, Maricela had felt left out. Like Aunt Cora said, when people act mean, they are often hurting inside. Sure, there were better ways to deal with the situation than to seek revenge, but it took courage to admit loneliness.

"I didn't—" Pru was about to defend herself again. Then she stopped, shoved her hands into her pockets, and took a deep breath. "Look, Maricela, you have to understand. You were always welcome to ride with us. But you never did."

"My mom wouldn't allow it. She said it was too dangerous and not ladylike."

"You still can ride with us," Abigail said. Then everyone, including Chica Linda and Boomerang, looked at Pru, waiting for her reaction.

"Seriously?" Pru asked. "I'm supposed to forget that she did all that stuff to me?" She groaned. "Yeah, I get it.

Forgiveness and all that." She sighed. "Okay, Maricela, yes, you are always welcome to go riding with us. Can we just stop fighting?"

Lucky smiled. They all knew how selfish Maricela could be, how calculating and unpleasant, and yet Pru had taken the high road and not only forgiven her, but was willing to include her. Pru was a good person and an amazing friend.

But before Maricela could reply, Abigail squealed. "Look," she said, pointing to the filly. "She's getting to her feet!"

31

By evening it was clear—the filly was going to be okay. She was not only walking around, but eating small amounts of hay. "We'll need to keep her for a day or two," Fanny Granger said. "Just to make sure she regains all her strength. But it looks like we got to her in the nick of time."

That was the best news ever.

As darkness fell, the mare returned to her herd. Lucky was glad that she'd be warm in the cave with the other mustangs, rather than outside in the cold. Did the mare understand that they were not keeping her baby? That they'd return her as soon as possible? Lucky hoped so. Spirit, however, ventured into the barn and kept close to the filly. "You're a good uncle," Lucky told him.

In times of crisis or times of celebration, the Granger kitchen was the usual gathering place for Pru and her family's guests, but on this night everyone was drawn back into the barn. Al and Jim brought lanterns, while Jacques and Fanny carried a large pot of hot cocoa.

Cora and Miss Flores helped ladle the cocoa into mugs. Then they all sat on bales of hay—even Maricela, who didn't once complain about how the animals smelled. As the stars twinkled through the windows, and Abigail's snowflakes dangled from the rafters, lantern light warmed the barn with an amber glow. The chickens, rabbits, sheep, and goats settled into their spaces. Chica Linda, Boomerang, Spirit, and the other horses seemed content, with eyes closed and ears relaxed. Even the filly, who'd curled onto a blanket, looked peaceful.

It was Miss Flores who spoke first. She tapped a spoon against her mug to get everyone's attention. "I wanted to say how very impressed I am with you girls. Your parents told me how hard you worked making the critter care packages. I think you each deserve an A for your winter project." Lucky, Pru, and Abigail, who were sitting together on a bale, smiled and happily elbowed one another. But Maricela, who was sitting by herself, raised her hand.

"Miss Flores?"

"Yes, Maricela?"

"I think you should know that I…" She looked down

at her mug. "That I…" Lucky was stunned. Was Maricela struggling to speak? She *always* had something to say. Pru stiffened, as did Lucky, expecting the worst. Was Maricela about to tell Miss Flores that she was the only one who deserved the A grade? Maricela swallowed hard, then looked up. "I didn't do as much work as the others. You should know that."

"I see." Miss Flores nodded slowly. "And why didn't you do as much work?" She didn't sound critical, just curious.

"Because…" Maricela hesitated. Was she going to tell everyone about her feelings? How she'd been mad at Pru all these years? How she'd felt left out, and friendless, and hurt? She'd already confessed all those feelings to the PALs, and wasn't that enough?

"Maricela helped with the filly," Lucky said. "She fed her medicine and soothed her. That was very helpful."

"Yes," Abigail said. "Very helpful."

Maricela's eyes widened with surprise. "But…?"

"We're a team," Pru explained. "We all deserve the same grade."

Lucky smiled with pride. She couldn't have said

it better herself. Did Maricela's confession mean that she'd changed her ways? Maybe. Or maybe not. Lucky knew that she couldn't control what Maricela said or did, but the PALs had done their best to make her feel welcome, and that was good enough for Lucky. She scooted closer to Pru, then looked at Maricela and patted the empty spot on the hay bale. Maricela walked across the barn and sat next to her.

"Then it's an A for the entire group," Miss Flores said.

Though the girls were quite gleeful at that moment, Jim and Al weren't smiling. They were staring at their daughters with concern. Al pushed back his hat. "While I'm proud of your schoolwork, don't get me wrong, there's still the matter of you two riding when I specifically told you not to," he said.

"You do realize that there will be punishment," Jim told them. "You know that, right?" Lucky nodded. As did Pru. That's when Abigail jumped to her feet.

"You have to punish me, too," she insisted. "Because I knew all about it and I was going to cover for them."

Al's scowl melted and he chuckled quietly. "You girls really are a team, aren't you?" On that note,

Jacques passed around a platter of freshly baked oatmeal cookies.

Pru gently pulled Abigail back onto the hay bale. "Are you crazy?" Pru whispered. "You didn't have to do that. He's gonna come up with something really bad, like digging holes for fence posts, or skinning rattlesnakes for his favorite soup."

"We're a team, remember?" Abigail said. She was about to eat her cookie when Boomerang snatched it from her hand. "Boomerang!"

When the cookies were gone and the cocoa consumed, everyone started to bundle up to leave. Cora pulled a pair of gloves from her pocket, then sat next to Lucky. "Don't think I didn't notice your hands, young lady."

Lucky turned her palms upward, revealing the chapped skin. "My gloves got wet from scooping snow, so my hands got a bit frozen."

"I have some of Dr. Merriweather's burn cream at home. It should take the sting away." She handed the gloves to Lucky. "For now, wear these." Both Lucky and Cora paused a moment, looking across the barn as Lucky's dad said good-bye to Miss Flores. It was one of those long, lingering good-byes. Cora reached out and squeezed Lucky's arm. She didn't need to say anything. Lucky knew what the squeeze meant. Change might be coming, but Cora would always be there for her, even if Lucky broke more rules, even if she refused to wear layers, even if their family's size and shape changed. And her father would always be there, too. "I love you," Cora said.

"I love you, too."

Change can be a scary thing. But after moving to a new town, sleeping in a new bed, making new friends, and learning new skills, Lucky knew she could handle whatever changes came her way. She walked over to Spirit and ran her hand down his muzzle. "Good night, boy," she said. "See you in the morning." He nodded, then lay next to the filly. Lucky took her father's hand and they started the walk home.

Most days are ordinary, filled with familiar sights, sounds, and practiced routines. But for Fortuna Esperanza Navarro Prescott, most days were *extra*ordinary. And she hoped it would always be that way.

32

Spirit dipped his head and gulped some cool, clear
water. Pools had formed here and there, thanks to the
melting snow. With each passing day, more birds were
returning, busily gathering twigs for their nest making.
It was nice to hear their songs once again. Grasses,
bright green and crisp, poked out of the thawing ground.
Rabbit families emerged from their burrows, their noses
and whiskers twitching. It was safe for them to venture
out, for the wolf pack had returned to the depths of the
forest. Spirit lifted his head and nodded at his sister,
who stood on the other side of the pool, her filly at her
side. Soon, the filly would be a yearling. She was healthy
and strong like her mother. The whole herd was healthy.
Spirit tossed his mane with pride. He'd known feelings of
love, of protection and of fear, but at that moment he was
blessed by the feeling of contentment.

"Spirit!"

He turned. Up on the ridge, the brown-and-white
pinto stood with his yellow-haired girl. The palomino
stood beside him, with her black-haired girl. And sliding
off the palomino's back was the brown-haired girl. Spirit's

girl. She waved and called his name again. He neighed to his herd, bidding them good-bye. Then he bolted up the trail, pausing only long enough for his girl to grab his mane and swing herself into place. She smelled like soap and oatmeal cookies.

But there was another scent, the one that arrived at this time every year. It was the scent of promises—that grasses would grow, that trees would fruit, and that life would renew. With Spirit in the lead, the horses and their girls took their first ride of spring.

Author's Note

Once again I've been blessed with an amazing project. Huge thanks to Kara Sargent at Little, Brown Books for Young Readers for inviting me to write these novels about Spirit the wild mustang and the girl who loves him. Kara and I share a love for animals, and so teaming up for a project like this seemed as natural as breathing.

There are many people to thank, for a writer never works alone. Sometimes it feels like some act of magic has occurred when the finished book actually arrives on my doorstep and I get to hold it for the first time. The magicians responsible for this story are, from Universal/DreamWorks Animation: Aury Wallington, Rich Burns, Laura Sreebny, Katherine Nolfi, Robert Taylor, Lauren Bradley, Megan Startz, Harriet Murphy, Corinne Combs, Barb Layman, Mike Sund, David Wiebe, Andrew Tolbert, Heather Oster, Rebecca Goldberg, Alex Ward, and Susan Weber; and from Little, Brown, working alongside Kara Sargent: Dani Valladares, Christina Quintero, Kristina Pisciotta, Lindsay Walter-Greaney, Dan Letchworth, Allegra Green, Carol Scatorchio, and Victoria Stapleton.

And a big thanks to Jeremy Bishop, Megan Chance, Sue and Faith Kerrigan, Vicky Poole, Michael Bourret, and to my family, Bob, Walker, and Isabelle.

I humbly offer each of them a heartfelt thanks.

Ride Free, everyone!

Turn the page for a sneak
peek at the adventure
that started it all

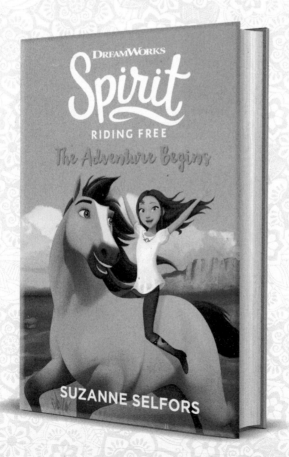

1

The morning sun streamed through the windows as
Lucky's shoes beat their wild rhythm.

Though Lucky was a natural runner, with long,
strong legs, the shoes themselves hadn't been designed
for such activity. Made from stiff black leather, with a
half-inch heel, they laced tightly up the shins. That very
morning the boots had been polished to a perfect sheen
by the family butler. If she kept running, Lucky would
surely develop blisters, but she didn't have far to go.

With no one around to witness, Lucky picked
up speed and darted down the hallway of Madame
Barrow's Finishing School for Young Ladies. Running
within school walls was strictly prohibited, along with
other disrespectful activities like pencil gnawing and
gum chewing. But sometimes rules had to be broken,
especially when a hot, buttered scone was at stake. So
Lucky ran as fast as she could, her long brown braid
thumping against her back. Morning tea at Barrow's was
a tradition the headmistress had brought with her from
England. The school's cook could make the pastry so
flaky it practically melted in the mouth. And she stuffed

each one with a huge dollop of salted butter and sweet blackberry jam. Lucky's mouth watered just thinking about it. But she was late. So very late. Which wasn't entirely her fault.

There'd been a…*distraction*.

She'd been looking out the window as she tended to do during morning recitations, her mouth moving automatically, for she knew her multiplication tables by heart. "Twelve times five is sixty. Twelve times six is seventy-two." Her legs felt twitchy, as they often did when she was forced to sit for long periods of time. "Twelve times seven is eighty-four. Twelve times eight is ninety-six."

"Lucky, please stop fiddling," the teacher said.

"Yes, ma'am." Lucky sat up straight and tucked her feet behind the chair legs to keep them still.

"Continue, everyone."

"Twelve times nine is—"

Lucky stopped reciting. Something on the other side of the street caught her eye. It was a horse, but not the usual sort that one saw in the city. This horse wasn't attached to a carriage or wagon. A bright-red blanket lay across his back and feathers hung from his black mane. He was being led down the sidewalk by a man whose long blond hair was topped by a cowboy hat. The fringe on the man's pants jiggled as he walked. Certainly the city was full of colorful people who came from every corner of the world, but Lucky had never seen a cowboy in person, only in photographs. He walked in a funny, bowlegged way and was handing out pieces of paper to passersby. Lucky leaned closer to the window, but a carriage pulled up and blocked her view.

"Twelve times fourteen is…" Lucky tapped her fingers on the desk. She couldn't get that cowboy and his beautiful horse out of her mind. What were they doing in the city?

"Lucky. Please sit still!"

And so it was that after recitations, instead of heading to tea with the other students, Lucky snuck out the front door to see if the cowboy was still there.

He wasn't. And by that time, morning tea had already begun.

The headmistress believed that teatime was as crucial to a young lady's education as literature or history because it taught manners and the important art of conversation. Plus, she insisted that the tea they served at Barrow's Finishing School was superior because it came all the way from England and had a picture of Queen Victoria on the tin. Lucky wasn't a huge fan of the stuff, but those scones were to die for.

She bounded up the flight of stairs, lifting her long skirt so she wouldn't get tangled. She detested the school uniform—a stiff white blouse that buttoned all the way to the chin and a gray wool skirt that always seemed too heavy and too hot. She'd pleaded many times for a change in uniform. She'd brought in newspaper articles to show the headmistress that pants were all the rage in other countries. But her reasonable request fell on deaf ears, for the headmistress was as immobile as a ship in the sand. "My young ladies will not be seen in public in a pair of bloomers!"

Lucky leaped onto the second-floor landing. From the end of the hall came the clinking of china and the quiet conversations of her fellow students. She was almost there. Still gripping her skirt, she dashed out of the stairwell, turned sharply on her heels, and then raced down the hall.

Only to bump into something.

Correction—into *someone*.

When a scone-craving, restless student collides with a no-nonsense, uppity headmistress, the impact is the stuff of legend. Not only was the wind knocked out of both parties, but they were thrown off-balance. Objects flew into the air—a notebook, a hair comb, a marble pen. When Lucky reached out to break her fall, she grabbed the first thing in front of her, which happened to be the headmistress's arm. Down they both tumbled, landing on the hallway carpet in a most unladylike way. Lucky knew this was bad—very bad. The headmistress had probably never sat on the ground in her entire life, let alone been knocked down to it!

Madame Barrow pushed a stray lock of hair from her eyes. "Fortuna. Esperanza. Navarro. Prescott!" she said between clenched teeth.

"Gosh, I'm so sorry," Lucky said, scrambling to her feet. "I didn't see you." She offered a hand to the headmistress, pulling her up off the carpet. Then she collected the hair comb, notebook, and pen. "Are you hurt?"

Madame Barrow, headmistress of Barrow's Finishing School for Young Ladies, did not answer the question. Instead, with expertly manicured fingers, she brushed carpet fuzz off her perfectly pressed gray skirt. She set her hair comb back into place, collected the pen and notebook, and then drew a focused breath, filling her lungs as if she were about to dive underwater. Lucky could have sworn that the intake of oxygen added another inch to the headmistress's towering frame. Silence followed. Agonizing silence. Then, after a long exhale, the headmistress spoke. "Do you know how long I have been teaching young ladies of society?" she asked in her thick British accent.

"No, Madame Barrow." Lucky tried not to stare at the headmistress's right eyelid, which had begun to quiver with rage.

"Fifteen years, Miss Prescott. Fifteen *dedicated* years." With a flourish of her hand, she began what Lucky expected would be a long, *dedicated* lecture. "I was raised and educated in England, Miss Prescott, a country that is the pillar of civility and tradition. The patrons of this institution have placed the tender education of their daughters in my capable hands. In my fifteen years here, I have encountered many different sorts of young ladies. But never, and I repeat, *never*, has one child exhibited so much…*spirited energy.*"

Spirited energy? Lucky fidgeted. "I know I'm not supposed to run, but—"

The headmistress held up a hand, stopping Lucky mid-excuse. A moment of uncomfortable silence followed. At the other end of the hall, a few students poked their heads out of the tearoom. Eavesdropping. Who could blame them? The scene in the hall was oodles more interesting than the idle chitchat they were forced to engage in while sipping tea. "Must I remind you that running *inside* is not appropriate behavior for a young lady of society?"

"Yes, Madame Barrow. I mean, no, you don't need to remind me." Lucky shuffled in place. Sarah Nickerson's head appeared next to the others. She smirked. Lucky wanted to holler, "Mind your own business, Sarah!" But she didn't.

"And yet...you ran." The headmistress raised an eyebrow. Lucky scratched behind her ear. She was starting to feel itchy, as if allergic to the headmistress's intense and unblinking gaze.

"I'm sorry?"

"Are you asking me if you're sorry?"

"Um, no, but it's just that..." Lucky's stomach growled. Loudly. "It's just that I didn't want to be late for morning tea."

"Come with me," the headmistress said. As she turned around, Sarah and the other eavesdroppers darted back into the tearoom. Lucky sighed. There'd be no scones today.

The headmistress's office contained lots of lovely things. A collection of china plates graced the walls, lace doilies draped every surface, and a pair of lovebirds twittered in a wicker birdcage.

"How many times have you visited my office this school year?" Madam Barrow asked as she settled into her desk chair.

"I'm not sure." Lucky had lost count.

"Eight times, Miss Prescott. *Eight times.*" Lucky nodded. The incidents streamed through her mind. She'd slid down the entry banister. She'd climbed a ladder to check out a bird's nest on a school windowsill. She'd eaten a cricket on a dare. And there was all the running. "I'm beginning to think that I'm sharing my office with you."

That was a funny thought. Lucky giggled, then tried to take it back but made a snorting sound instead. "Sorry." It was a well-known fact that Madam Barrow did not possess a sense of humor.

The headmistress tapped her fingers on her desk. She seemed more upset than usual, sitting as if a plank were tied to her back. Lucky hadn't been invited to sit, so she stood just inside the doorway, doing her best not to fidget. "This is a finishing school, Miss Prescott. Do you know what that means?"

Of course she did. She'd heard the motto hundreds of times. "Preparing Young Ladies for Society."

"Correct. Young ladies, such as you, enter this school as unformed little lumps of clay. Under my guidance and the tutelage of your teachers, you are shaped—formed—into finished works of art." She smiled, but there was no warmth in the expression.

Lucky didn't like to think of herself as a lump of clay—or a lump of anything. And she was not quite sure why she had to be turned into a work of art. Works of art were stuck in museums, behind glass or on pedestals. Works of art stayed in one place. That was much worse than being stuck in recitations.

The headmistress opened her desk drawer and took out a piece of writing paper. Then, using her marble pen, she began to write. She paused a moment, glanced up. "You've put me in a difficult position. Are you aware of this?"

"I didn't mean to." Lucky felt a tingle on her ankle, the beginning of a blister. Those shoes were really the worst. Why did every part of her uniform have to be so stiff? She shifted her weight, trying to find relief.

"Are you listening to me?" the headmistress asked.

"Yes." Lucky stopped moving. "I won't run anymore.

Really, I won't. I mean, not inside. Unless there's a fire. I have to run if there's a fire. Or an earthquake."

The headmistress sighed. "Miss Prescott, I want all my students to succeed, but I'm beginning to question your chances."

That sounded very serious. Lucky didn't set out to break the rules or to test the headmistress's patience. It just happened. "I know. I'm really sorry. Truly I am. But I saw this cowboy outside and I wanted to…" Leaving school without a parent or guardian was strictly prohibited, and by admitting this, she'd just made things worse.

The headmistress turned red, as if she'd painted rouge over her entire face. "I find I am near my wits' end. How can I be expected to put up with such continued willfulness?"

Willfulness? Lucky wondered. Was it willful to want to see a real, live cowboy up close? Was it willful to want to get somewhere quickly? Was it willful to want a scone? If so, then why was being willful such a bad thing? The problem, in Lucky's opinion, was that there were too many rules and way too much sitting. She couldn't help that her legs got twitchy.

The headmistress began writing again.

"I didn't mean to bump into you. I'm sorry, I really am." Lucky leaned forward. "What are you writing?"

The headmistress wrote a few more lines, then signed her name with a flourish. After folding the paper, she applied a blob of wax and pressed the school's seal into it. "The question you must ask yourself, Fortuna, is *What am I made of?*" She held out the letter. "Please deliver this to your father after school. You are dismissed."

Lucky reluctantly took the letter and was about to head out the door when the headmistress cleared her throat. *Oh, that's right*, Lucky thought. She turned back around and said, "Thank you, Ma'am." The headmistress nodded. Then Lucky made her escape.

On previous occasions, upon leaving the headmistress's office, Lucky had felt a wave of relief. But never before had the headmistress said she was at her wits' end. And never before had she written a letter with a secret message to Lucky's father. There could be nothing good in that letter.

Fortuna Esperanza Navarro Prescott fought the urge to run as she tucked what she believed to be her doom into her pocket.

2

Lucky stood in the hallway as the other students streamed out of the tearoom. Most greeted her with sympathetic smiles, for Lucky was well liked at school. Only Sarah Nickerson stopped to gloat. "In trouble again? When are you going to realize that you don't belong here?" Sarah asked. But she didn't wait for an answer. Lucky wouldn't have bothered anyway. It was no use trying to talk to someone like Sarah, who'd been taught by her parents that because one side of Lucky's family didn't "come from money," Lucky wasn't Sarah's social equal.

As the hallway cleared, the last student to emerge from the tearoom was Emma Popham. Emma had a sneaky look on her face. She glanced around, then slipped a scone into Lucky's hand. "Thanks," Lucky whispered, then ate the scone in two bites. She and Emma always looked out for each other.

After wiping crumbs off her lips, Lucky grabbed the handles of Emma's rolling chair, a fancy chair with wheels that allowed Emma to move about. As a little girl, Emma had suffered a sickness that left her legs skinny and weak. She could stand for short periods, but she couldn't walk more than a few steps.

"So I heard," Emma said as Lucky wheeled her down the hallway, "you were in the headmistress's office."

"I'm setting a school record."

Emma placed her hands over a pair of books that lay in her lap. "Did Madame Barrow remind you that"—she conjured a British accent for the rest of the sentence—"you're a little lump of clay that needs to be molded into a work of art?"

"Actually, she told me that *you're* the lump."

"No, you are."

"No, you are." They both laughed.

One of the nice things about going to the most prestigious school in the city was that the school came complete with all the latest technologies, including an elevator. Lucky opened the elevator gate, then the door, and pushed Emma into the small chamber before stepping inside behind her. She turned the lever. After a loud clanking sound and a quick jarring motion, the elevator moved slowly upward.

Lucky leaned against the wall. "Madame Barrow wrote a letter to my dad."

"What does it say?"

"I don't know. But I'm guessing it's not good. Something about me being *willful* and having too much *spirited energy.*"

"Well, that's better than having a stick up your behind like Sarah," Emma said. "Besides, your dad won't get mad. He never gets mad at you. He adores you." Emma was trying to make Lucky feel better, but Lucky's stomach tightened with worry. She didn't want to disappoint her father. "Why were you late, anyway?"

"I saw a cowboy and a horse with feathers in his mane!"

"Really?"

"Yes, really. Walking down the street. The cowboy was passing out pieces of paper to people and I wanted to see what it was all about."

"Did you get one?"

"No." Though she still wanted answers about the cowboy and his horse, she couldn't shake her worry about the letter. "What if Madame Barrow wants to kick me out of the school?"

"Never," Emma said with a wave of her hand. "She wouldn't do that."

"But what if the letter's really bad and Dad decides I need some kind of punishment?"

Emma shrugged. "It's really not a big deal. If he does punish you, then he'll do what my parents always do. He'll make you stay home on weekends and not go to any—" She gasped. "Oh no. You don't think he'll make you miss *my* party?"

The elevator had reached the third floor, but Lucky didn't open the door right away. Emma's question hung in the air over both their heads, like a storm cloud.

Emma's birthday party was going to be the most glorious party ever. At least that's how Lucky imagined it. The Pophams lived in a stone mansion on Church Street, with a private stable for their carriage horses. No expense would be spared for the event. Emma's perfumed invitations had been mailed weeks ago. "I'm going to your party," Lucky said as she opened the elevator door. "I'll do chores for the rest of my life if I have to. I'll help with the shopping and the cooking. Nothing's going to stop me." She grabbed the handles and wheeled Emma out of the elevator.

"And I'll help you with those chores," Emma said. "Because there's no way I'm turning thirteen without my best friend."

Library was next on the schedule. According to Madame Barrow, young ladies should always take time to properly digest a meal, so after enjoying tea and scones, they faced another long bout of sitting. But Lucky didn't mind, because she loved reading. Adored it, in fact. For a young lady of society, reading was the only socially approved type of exploration.

The school library took up most of the third floor. Bookshelves lined the walls, and embroidered cushions decorated the velvet chairs. A fire usually crackled in the winter, but on this spring day the window was open, permitting a nice breeze. Lucky wheeled Emma to their favorite corner, by a window that overlooked the park. Emma held up the books she'd been cradling on her lap. "Dad got these for us. They're both by Jules Verne. I can't wait to start this one. *Twenty Thousand Leagues Under the Sea.*" She and Lucky were drawn to the same kind of stories—grand adventures in exotic locations, brimming with danger. This was one of the many reasons why they were best friends.

"Oh, I've read that one," Lucky said. "Everyone thinks there's this huge sea monster, and they send out these guys to kill it, but the sea monster turns out to be a—"

"Don't tell me the whole story!" Emma cried.

"Oops." Lucky smiled. "Trust me, you're gonna love it." She grabbed the other book. "*Journey to the Center of the Earth.* This looks great."

"You can keep it."

"Thanks."

The clock struck eleven. The other students found seats, and everyone took out their books and began to read. Along with the clock's ticking and pages rustling, young children squealed in the park, but none of those sounds distracted Lucky. The only time she didn't get squirmy was when her nose was stuck in a book. *How does one get to the center of the earth?* she wondered. Was there a secret tunnel? She'd never been outside the city, except to go to her grandfather's country house upstate. Lucky opened to the first page, ready for another story to take her someplace amazing.

A shadow fell across the page. Mrs. Beachwood, a portly woman with a jiggly chin and a warm smile, had wandered over. "I see you two are sticking with the adventure genre."

"Yes," Emma said.

Was that a twinkle in Mrs. Beachwood's eye? "Wouldn't you prefer a gentler story? A story about taking care of your home?" She held up a book titled *The Joys of Domestic Duties*. Emma and Lucky cringed. "Or perhaps this one?" The second choice was *Manners and Etiquette of a Young Lady*. Because it had been written by the headmistress, it had been read by most of the students. Lucky groaned to herself. The corners of Mrs. Beachwood's eyes crinkled in amusement. "I see how it is. You'd rather read about dangerous places, courageous heroes, and evil villains than about how to tell a salad fork from a dessert fork."

"Yes!" they both said, forgetting the quiet rule.

Mrs. Beachwood cupped a hand around the side of her mouth and whispered, "Well, I wholly approve." Then she began to shelve books.

Lucky curled up in her chair and opened to the first chapter. She always felt a rush of excitement when she began a new book. Where was she going? What would she see? Would this story give her nightmares or would it make her laugh? She felt restless again, but it wasn't her legs. The feeling came from a deeper place. Lucky didn't fully understand yet, but what she felt at that moment was longing. There are people who never have this feeling, people who are content to stay put. But Lucky longed to go somewhere. Maybe not to the center of the earth, maybe not twenty thousand leagues under the sea, but somewhere.

Somewhere beyond her tidy, inside life.

Join the adventure with Lucky and Spirit!

Kirkus calls DreamWorks *Spirit Riding Free: The Adventure Begins,*

"A wild ride that will make spirits soar."

Share your thoughts using #ReadSpirit